—P

"In many ways, it seems only yesterday that I stood atop the aeries of the Avakhar and watched a blood-red sun die in the seas of Indrae. Yet, much has passed since then. I have crossed the Great Wastes and lived to tell it. I have captured the terrible Sentinel of Man. I have betrayed the Lord Tharrin's trust and loosed an awesome force upon the world.

"And, as ever, woven within every great tapestry are threads of little consequence: I have made a fool of myself several times over. I have been peed upon by the largest creature in the world. I have won the love of fair Corysia, and lost a perfectly good ear in the doing.

"Great deeds and small, then. Each has its place in the scheme of things, or so the Avakhar would have us believe. Perhaps this is true, though I cannot give credence to all that I heard in the towers of Indrae. It is difficult to trust creatures who crack lice with their beaks, and believe they are yet unborn.

"Still, I suppose I have little room to talk about wisdom in others. I have seen things no other person on Earth has even dreamed. I have been given a knowledge older than all of history. I have even come face to face with the spectre of myself. Yet, for all these wonders, I have gained little understanding. And I can say in all honesty that I have no heart for the fearsome task before me . . ."

> —Aldair, late of the Venicii, aboard the free vessel *Ahzir al'Rhaz*

ALDAIR, MASTER OF SHIPS

≈≈≈≈≈≈≈≈≈≈≈≈≈≈≈≈≈≈≈

by
Neal Barrett, Jr.

DAW BOOKS, INC.
DONALD A. WOLLHEIM, PUBLISHER

1301 Avenue of the Americas
New York, N. Y.   10019

FIRST PRINTING, SEPTEMBER 1977

1 2 3 4 5 6 7 8 9

PRINTED IN U.S.A.

ONE

It is well known that the Vikonen are afraid of nothing on earth save an empty belly, though I know for certain there is one thing more that strikes fear in their hearts. It is believed among the Northmen that a warrior who perishes on dry soil is doomed for a thousand years to the seven hells of Rhagnir. There, his soul lingers in agony with the smells of the sea and good barley beer to taunt him. It is no small wonder the Vikonen are fearless fighters on the land, as well as masters of the sea.

Thus, I read only displeasure in the broad features of Signar-Haldring as we kept our long night vigil. He was decidedly unhappy so many leagues from salt water, but he was not afraid—even this close to the forests of the Lauvectii.

He was, however, sorely vexed with me. For it was my doing that had brought us to this place, and he had let me know more than once that he would not think highly of me if we chanced to die here.

"Old friend," I said, after we had squatted in the cold some time without speaking, "your thoughts are dark enough to choke vipers, if any are about at this hour. I would just as soon hear your grumblings as wonder at them."

When he turned to me, I could see glints of starlight in stone-agate eyes. The night was chill with autumn's bite, and specks of hoarfrost tipped his furry ears and the hairs of his thick black pelt.

"It may be that you would not, Aldair. My thoughts are somewhat less than pleasant."

5

"I am not surprised to hear this."

His nose twitched irritably. "What would you have me say, then? I can only tell you what I have said before. This is not a good place to be. I do not like the color of the land. I most certainly do not care for the smell of it. It reeks of old meat."

"Those are hares hanging from a tree somewhere," I told him. "A Stygiann will eat nearly anything he can catch, and he is always hungry. But if there is meat to spare, he will wedge it in a branch to age, and come back for it."

The Vikonen made a face. "That is a disgusting habit."

"I agree. But a Stygiann finds the aroma of rotting hare most inviting. There is no accounting for taste in this world. Rheif was ever sticking up his nose at my desire for fresh vegetables. Rooty-things and weeds, he used to say. And when we were slaves of the Nicieans, we were both repelled by the noxious beetle stew those creatures favor."

"In your thoughts of food," growled Signar, "you have no doubt forgotten what Stygianns like even better than hares."

"That is hardly likely," I reminded him. "I was born in the Eubirones, and I am no stranger to Stygiann ways."

"Sometimes, one wonders."

I turned and faced him squarely. "All right. Say what is in your mind."

The big warrior made a noise in his chest. "Nothing is in my mind that has not been there before. Aldair, you cannot expect every Stygiann to be as *he* was. I have not forgotten that Rheif was a brother to us both. Those creatures out there are not my brothers. Or yours. It is not the same."

"Nothing is the same as it was," I said. Signar didn't answer, for he knew the truth of that as well as I.

Past us, beneath the crest of our small hillock, the land sloped gently under short grasses to the edge of the Lauvectii. It is not a woodland that begins slowly, or by degree. It is very abruptly there, a dark and sudden wall of ancient oaks so thick upon themselves that little sun reaches the forest floor, even in the full light of day. Much is told of this lair of the Stygianns. Most of it is untrue, for few have ventured into these woods and come out again. The Rhemian legions, having conquered half the world, want nothing to do with this place. The soldier of the Empire is a worthy foe as long as his enemies will line up properly and fight in a civilized manner— but he does not like to crawl about in wet, unfriendly forests. It is said that Stygianns are fond of catching legionaries in

full armor, and find it amusing that a fine fat meal would wear
its own pot for cooking. It may be this is true—but I greatly
doubt it.

Personally, I see no need to make up foolish tales about
these creatures. They are fierce and cunning in their own
right, and I cannot blame Signar for being uncomfortable this
close to their homeland. It is no reflection upon his courage.
A person gets used to his own brand of danger, and is un-
easy with another.

While I watched, a faint patch of pearl-colored sky touched
the far horizon. In moments, I could see the leaden waters of
the River Rheinus behind our hill, and beyond that, the lands
of Gaullia, still in darkness. I have seldom been happier to
see a morning, being cold clear through to the bone. My snout
was near frozen, and I could no longer feel my ears. At the
time I would have gladly traded my own sparse coat of hair for
Signar's great black pelt. At least, until the spring.

Squinting into the valley, I tried to see where my arrow had
found its mark, but darkness still blurred the new morning.
Only a Stygiann has eyes to strain one shadow from another.

"It will soon be light," Signar grumbled beside me. "They
will spot us for certain, Aldair, squatting like stones out here
in the open."

I tried to hide my amusement. "They have known we were
here, friend, since we first set foot across the river."

Signar frowned, showing big white teeth like stubby daggers.
"You have seen them, then?"

"It is not a thing I have to see. They are Stygianns."

He bristled and sniffed the air, turning his furry muzzle to
the wind. "Then we are done for—unless we forget this foolishness and make for the river.'

"We have already spoken of this," I reminded him. "It is a
thing that must be done."

The deep rumble within his chest told me what he thought
about that.

One moment there was nothing, only the mottled curtain of
deepest olive and the tangle of weighty branches. And then he
was there, gaunt and gray against the forest. Signar stiffened
beside me.

"No, it's all right. He has come."

"Someone has," he said dryly. "And how many more behind him?"

I didn't answer. Standing, where the creature could see me, I loosed my blade-belt and let it fall to the ground. Then I picked up the long sacked bundle and started down the hill. Like so many things, since my life has become more than my own, I knew this was a moment that had to be. Signar knew this too, for he is aware of where I have been, and what I have seen there. But knowing a thing is not always the same for one as it is for another.

Stygianns never change. They have a pride beyond all other creatures, and are stubborn as stones. They show great disdain for all things that happen in the world beyond the Lauvectii—yet, in truth, they are as curious as children. The fellow who waited for me now leaned lazily against a tree, gazing off to the north as if he had no idea that I was there. Still, I knew his dark red eyes were ever upon me, and I did not make the mistake of approaching too closely.

"R'tai. Mahr a shinn, Stygiaar."

He looked up at my words, studying me over a long, pointed muzzle. He was lean and rangy—fur gray as shadow covered a hard sheath of muscle that wound like a rope about every inch of his frame. If he was surprised I spoke his tongue, he was determined not to show it. "I am Aldair, of clan Venicii," I told him.

"Interesting," said the Stygiann. He opened his mouth in amusement, showing me sharp teeth and a red tongue. "I did not know till now the word *char'desh* had names."

I knew the word, which simply means *food.* "Why not, Stygiann? If boots can have names, so can a meal."

His smile faded, and strong cords gathered in his shoulders. He had not missed the hide of his brothers on my feet. "Strange words, from a creature who comes unarmed to the woods of the Lauvectii. Are you tired of your stay in this world, little warrior?"

"If my life is in danger here, so is the honor of the Stygianns."

He laughed at that, the peculiar coughing sound that passes for laughter among his kind. "This is foolishness, *char'desh.* There is most certainly honor among the Stygiaar, but the word can have no meaning between our people and other creatures. It would not be seemly."

"It would, if that honor concerned a warrior-brother who has perished in a far place, without a kinsman to hear his prayers."

Anger flushed his features. "What can you know of such things? It does me great dishonor to speak in this manner!"

. I looked into his eyes and did not turn away. "Stygiann, can we forget this foolishness for a moment? I loosed an arrow into this tree before the sun died, and I have been waiting atop that hill through the night, as you know. The arrow is gone, and so is the ring which it carried, though I see it now upon your finger. If you were not Rheif's kinsman you would have no right to wear it, and would not. I do you honor by returning it. Rheif is dead. I buried him in your own manner, with his blade in his hand and his eyes open to his enemies. I would have returned the rings of Khairi and Whoris, his brothers, but they died some time before him, and rest beneath the sea."

The Stygiann shook his head. "Now I am certain you are lying. No Lord of the Lauvectii would be fool enough to cross water."

"It was a necessity. They were not pleased about it."

"More than that, it never happened. Rheif and his brothers were taken by Rhemian soldiers. This is known to us."

"Rheif was taken. His brothers set him free. Through circumstances I will not recount, I found myself fleeing the Rhemians as well. We escaped together. Rheif's brothers were slain, but he and I ventured to far lands, and suffered much. We became friends, and brothers. I owe him my life, for he gave his own for me."

The Stygiann shifted his stance, and licked his muzzle thoughtfully. "It is true that you have returned the ring," he admitted darkly. "Why, I cannot say, for I believe nothing else you have told me. If anything, this is some trick or other to bring death to more warriors."

"I do not find it unnatural that a Stygiann would think first of treachery, instead of honor," I told him. "As for what you believe or do not believe, this is not a thing I can change. I have brought your kinsman's ring to rest. It is there on your finger—a logic that even a Stygiann cannot ignore. You may stand beneath a tree all day and wonder why a stone cannot fly, as I have seen your warriors do. You can play the fool with me and pretend I do not exist, or that the people of the Eubirones lack the sense to name themselves. Whatever you do—or choose not to do—will change nothing."

If I had had the speed to run at that moment, it might have been well to do so. A Stygiann's features may tell you nothing, but his thick bushy tail quite often reveals his intentions. This one's member flicked me a nervous warning that set my hairs on end. The clanfolk of the Eubirones are no cowards; we have bested Stygianns in battle before, and kept them from our lands for as long as anyone can remember. But we are no match for them in single combat. A Stygiann is neither as tall nor as broad as a Vikonen—but even the largest of my people are hardly more than chest-high to the Lords of the Lauvectii. We are squat and stubby-legged, and not made for running. We fight best in groups of three or more behind good blades. Or better still, with a fine bow of ash and a quiver of arrows—for there are no better archers in all of Gaullia.

However, I had neither of these weapons with me at the moment. Only a rather active mouth, which was beginning to wear upon this warrior.

The Stygiann scratched his chest and looked at me in wonder. "That is the longest speech I have ever heard. Is it over?"

"There is one thing more."

"There is, indeed. Your parting, while you are able. For I have decided it is too early in the day for killing."

I ignored this, as best I could. "As you have noticed, I brought something with me. It was meant for Rheif. Before I could present it to him, he was gone. Now, it is yours."

The Stygiann looked appalled. "Do you think me a fool? Nothing you could bring to the Lauvectii would be worth seeing."

"No doubt," I nodded, "and since you do not wish to see it, I will tell you that it is a blade—but a blade like none you have seen before. Its hilt is of gold, and it is set about with gems. There is no other like it in the world. It will cleave a small oak, or the strongest of armor."

This is one of the few moments I have seen a Stygiann without words. "I have no regard for your kind," he said finally. "That would be unseemly. But I did not till now know there was madness among the Eubirones."

I smiled, in spite of myself. He was proud and stubborn and as foolish as any of his kind. He would murder me in my tracks if the mood struck him. Or simply turn and walk away if a bee buzzed 'round his head and he decided to follow its path. That is the manner of Stygianns. Yet, I could see good Rheif in this fellow's eyes, and I remembered much.

"There is no doubt madness among the Eubirones," I said, "for there is madness upon all the world today. It is a time when day is night, and truth false. It is even a time when enemies are friends—though you cannot believe this now."

"I believe one thing. That I have had my fill of talk." He pulled himself up tall and laid a hand carelessly over the pommel of his blade. "I do not want that thing. Go back across the river, and take it with you. *My* gift to you is your life—I lose no honor in that, as there is little value in it."

I said nothing, but turned and left him there. But I did not take the blade back with me. I had not expected him to show interest while I was there, but he would soon be into its coverings. That, too, is the way of Stygianns.

Still, I would have given a silver piece to see his face, when he learned what was wrought upon the hilt of that great weapon.

TWO

It is relatively easy to glance at a stranger in Gaullia and know where he is from and what he does. We are not like our Rhemian cousins, who take great pleasure in looking alike. We have long been conquered by these people, but we have kept our own ways, for the most part. Thus, the Aeduii will ever seem as wheelers, whatever their trade. And to me, the people of Danuvvium continue to smell of fish, even though they have forsaken both the trade and traditional yellow smock of their forefathers.

It is much the same with all the folk of Gaullia. Merchants in the south still clip the bristles from their jowls and tend to fat, while the females of that region do not feel fully dressed until every breast is colored with powders, though none but their husbands—presumably—will see this wonder.

We are set in our ways, and fight change as if it were a plague. This is good in some ways, and bad in others—for there are benefits and comforts to be derived from Rhemian culture, if one does not mind paying the price. Most of us, though, appear to mind a great deal.

You could not guess that the conqueror had ever set foot in the city of Duroctium—mainly, because he seldom has before now. Duroctium lies close to the river, and the country-side is a favorite raiding ground for Stygianns. The people here are neither fat nor lazy, and they do not take kindly to those who are. Signar was greatly displeased that I had chosen to visit this place, particularly since it was uncommonly full of soldiers. I assured him they would not recognize me—that if they were looking at all, they would be looking for a warrior of the Venicii, which I did not appear to be at the moment. Moreover, I would not have a hulking giant beside me to draw undue attention.

He bristled at that. "By damn—you may wish you did if one of those kettle-heads gets a blade up your rear! I don't like the idea—them bein' where they shouldn't, and I can see no good reason for it, 'less it's us."

"They're watching for a *ship*," I reminded him, "a hundred leagues from here."

"Maybe, and maybe not," he growled. For a moment, his ears went flat against his skull, and he cautiously sniffed the air. By this, I was supposed to imagine we were in imminent danger of our lives. All I could see, however, were the flat towers of Duroctium through a break in the trees, the earthen walls turned dark as lead under a chill autumn sky.

"I do not intend to invade the city," I assured him. "We will be on our way by midday, or a little after."

Signar grunted, and pretended to mind our horses, which were in need of nothing, and content to nibble the dry grasses beneath the trees.

Though I have no great love for cities, it was pleasant to walk familiar streets again. Duroctium is not so far from my own lands—both the Bituraii and the Venicii are clans of the broad Eubirones Valley, and have much in common. My plain woolen cloak and thick breeches were the same as any other on the narrow cobbled ways. My sword was in Signar's care, as well as the blouse and jacket in clan colors. Either might have attracted more attention than I cared for.

It was a chill day, but cold never closed the markets of Gaullia. Farmers and merchants huddled over their wares, closing the way till two shoppers abreast could scarcely pass one another. This is the custom everywhere, even among Niceans across the Southern Sea.

Past market is a street called Ambergate, for no apparent reason. It winds beneath the shadow of the walls on one side, and crowded shops on the other. At its end, Cygnian slaves are bought and sold. There is no need to direct strangers to this place; even the most insensitive snout will find it. There were four of the poor brutes chained to posts before a shabby stall. Their heavy coats of winter wool were ragged and filthy.

They bleated to themselves and rolled their eyes, and for want of anything better to do, defecated on the ground.

My feelings about Cygnians—and slavery in general—have changed considerably over the past few years. There is nothing like wearing a chain yourself to broaden one's views on the subject. It is a frightening thing to be at the will of another, even a kindly master.

Thus, I hurried past this place, not particularly caring where I was going, and nearly blundered into a street filled with soldiers. They didn't see me, for they were intent on pestering some other poor soul. Some merchant, no doubt, who felt Rhemians should pay for their wares the same as any other. There were a dozen or so, soldiers on horseback wearing breastplates and tunics, and red tufted helmets on their heads. As they were cavalry, each fellow carried a longsword and a lance, instead of the short, stubby gladius.

This is all I remember about them. In truth, if the Emperor himself had been on hand, I would scarcely have noticed, for I could not take my eyes off the girl. Here was the reason for such a show of strength in Duroctium. If she had been mine, I would have guarded her as well. She was a vision. Pure delight. Rhemian, and highborn, but leaner than most of her kind. Black liquid eyes were set close above a perky little snout tipped with pink. Her body was covered with fine auburn hair, and there was much of it to see, for she shunned her cloak, even on this chilly day. The green satin gown that fell about her shoulders curved to her belly in neat half circles, barely concealing the soft row of breasts on either side.

Suddenly, I knew this beauty's eyes were on me, as well. That cold, haughty gaze that further chilled the morning told me she knew exactly what I was thinking. I flushed and turned away, feeling the fool. A woman always has this power. She can turn a male as hard as stone, or soft as jelly, and most delight in practicing both of these arts.

Old Galiun was ever a favorite of mine, perhaps because he had a penchant for fishing in quiet brooks, while my other uncles believed a boy should spend good summer days in the fields. He seemed old to me then, but not truly older now. He opened the door and saw me there, flung his arms wide and took me to him.

"Aldair, Creator's Eyes, you're the last person on earth I expected to see!"

"Uncle, it has been a while."

He held me from him, shaking his grizzly jowls in wonder. "Damn me, you're not a child, now, are you? Aldair, we thought you might be dead. Your mother——"

"There was a letter, uncle. Surely it came to her?"

"Aye, it did," he assured me. "But such a letter it was." He gave me a quick frown of disapproval. "Not the sort of thing to ease a mother's mind, or the rest of your kin."

He was right enough in that. "Uncle, there was little more I could do. After what happened, it would have been folly to make my way home, and bring trouble to the clan. Mother knows I didn't do the things I am accused of. In the letter——"

Galiun grinned and held up a hand. "Aldair—there's not a dozen could've done the things we've heard. Not in a single lifetime!"

"They came, then. From Silium."

"They did. A Good Father of the Church, and two fat legionaries, askin' where you might be and all, and of course we told them nothing, and couldn't have if we'd cared to. Aldair——" He cast a stern eye my way, in the manner of a good uncle. "You must see your mother. A word from me's not enough, if that's what you're asking."

My heart sank. He was right, and there was nothing I wanted more. "Uncle, I cannot."

"And *why* not?" he demanded. "You got to Duroctium. It's two days ride, maybe."

"Uncle——"

He peered at me closely, one old eye half closing. Then he rose to set cups and a pot of wine between us. "If there's trouble, you've got friends and family."

"It's not that kind of trouble. It's a thing I must do myself."

Galiun muttered, but said nothing. He was an old warrior, wise in the ways of honor. He might not approve, but he understood.

I downed the wine and stood, clasping his shoulders. "Tell her I love her, uncle. That I would come if I could. Tell her that much has happened to me, that I have been to far places, and will likely travel further still. And tell her that whatever she may have heard, I have brought no dishonor to the Venicii."

Galiun scowled fiercely. "Damn, boy, she knows that. Do you think we've come to believe Rhemians over our own?"

We held each other. I said no more, nor did uncle. There is no need for parting words among family. And indeed, this was well. What could I say that he would want to know? I could hear bells tolling in the church; it was mid-morning call, which sends up prayers for the souls of the dead in Albion. Could I tell him that? How I had stood on Albion's shores and seen no dead souls at all? That something far more terrifying than long-forgotten cousins haunted that place?

The Lord Tharrin was right: the truth is the very last thing people want to hear.

Away from Galiun's door, and into Lowbridge, I avoided the congestion of market—and more than that, the place where I had last seen Rhemian horse. I would've given much to glimpse the girl again, but this was not the time for such pleasures. I was nearly to the gates, then, and out of Duroctium, when the soldier stopped me.

"You there!"

I pretended not to hear, but he was having none of that. I turned to face him, and found four fine troopers instead of one. The first rider brought his mount up easily until his lance was half a meter from my chest.

"Citizen, do you have bad ears? By damn, I called you more than once!"

"Sir, it may be that I do," I told him. "I was injured something bad as a child, and don't always have my wits about me. Or so they say."

He leaned down toward me and grinned. "That may be. No one with their senses would live in such a dismal land. Now—" He sat up, and brought the lance closer. "—tell me who you are and where it is you're going."

"Cotus is my name, and I am going to Visius, which is my home."

The soldier frowned. "I have not heard of this Visius."

I gave him my best foolish smile. "It is quite small and insignificant."

"Possibly. Or possibly it simply doesn't exist."

"Some would say it is nearly small enough, sir."

"And what might you do in this—whatever?"

Behind him, his three friends edged up their mounts to listen. It was becoming a little crowded.

"Lout!" A lance prodded me in the stomach. "I asked you a question!"

"Sir! I am a—farmer. Nothing more. And not a very good one at that. If I plant corn, grasses grow in its place. If I plant for grasses, weeds come up instead. But there is nothing for it, since I have no other trade."

Two of the fellow's companions were grinning. The other was not. He was a short, grizzled campaigner, who had seen a few good fights in his time and would not mind finding another. "Stumbaucius," he said flatly, "ask this *farmer* if he always wears the boots of a warrior when he plants his grasses. I would like to hear his answer."

It was an extremely good question, and it taught me not to cast all Rhemians in the same lot, for a few appear to know our customs. How could I have taken such pains—and forgotten about the boots? There was little time for wonder. Behind me, I could hear the rest of this party rounding the corner, not half a block away. Soon I would have a full dozen legionaries on hand, few of which would be greatly amused by my farmer story.

The soldier's lance still pressed hard against me, and I counted my luck. The old campaigner would not have let it rest there—he had not stayed alive this long by offering weapons to his enemies. Slipping quickly aside, I grabbed it above the blade with both hands and jerked hard. The soldier grunted, staring with surprise at empty gauntlets. The others came at me and I tossed the weapon at the legs of their horses and ran.

—Not for the walls, or the alleys of the city. It is foolish to race a troop of Rhemian cavalry. Instead, I headed straight for the other riders coming up behind, screaming and shouting and waving my hands about wildly—a practice horses do not particularly care for.

"Stygianns!" I yelled, mingling with as many animals as possible, "Stygianns on the walls! Creator save us!"

The leader of this band stared at me, then his face went suddenly pale. Slapping his mount he bolted forward, his troopers close behind. Two soldiers held to guard the female, but they were slow to take their places, and not expecting trouble from the ground. I pulled myself up beside her, jerked the reins away and hauled the beast around. Both the lady and the horse screamed in protest, but I ignored them, making for the gates of Duroctium as quickly as possible.

~~~~~~~~~~~~~~~~~~

THREE

~~~~~~~~~~~~~~~~~~

Signar-Haldring has seen more than one altercation in his life, and it was not necessary to explain that he was now well into another. The sight of my kicking and shouting ladyfriend, doing her best to fly off a mount that was clearly not my own, told him more than he cared to know. For all his size, he moves incredibly fast when he has to. He was on his great mount with my own in tow before words could pass between us. The female saw him, and doubled her outcries. We know the Vikonen in the north, for they inhabit the cold lands above us, but I suppose they are an unusual sight for a Rhemian lady.

Signar stared at her with obvious irritation. "I assume there are others close behind? This is usually the case."

I glanced over my shoulder down the road. "An even dozen, I think. Less than a minute away."

"I gather you did not make friends in the city."

"This is clearly a failing of mine," I admitted.

"So it appears." He jerked his mount around, trotted a few paces into the wood, then hurried back. "A dozen it is. Six are right behind, under the hill. The others are circling off to the right and through the meadow—"

"—to cut us off on the road ahead," I finished. Without further words, we slapped our mounts and tore through low brush into the forest. We were of one mind. The road from Duroctium led west through flat and easy country—a boon to the Rhemians, and sure disaster for us. If we could cut through

the woods and circle past the city, we might lose them in the
hills to the east, then make our way back west, and to the sea.

Clearly, the lady saw no merit in this plan. With her
shouting and thrashing about, it was all I could do to keep
us both in the saddle.

"You will have to stop that," I told her. "It is difficult
enough riding through heavy forest, and it does not to have a
squirming creature abroad."

"Creature!" She exploded in a whole new fit of rage. "Lout,
do you think I intend to *help* you? I will have your *head* is
what I will do!"

'But if I let you go, you will intercede for me."

"Yes, yes!" She brightened suddenly. "I promise!"

"That is very amusing. Excuse me if I don't believe it—I
have had some experience with Rhemian promises."

What followed was a great deal of pummeling and scratching, and a long string of curses which did not fit her breeding.
I had little time to answer. Signar's great voice bellowed in
rage ahead. This, followed by cries of alarm and the ring of
iron on iron. Clutching the lady securely, I plunged through
a thicket of alders into a tight little clearing. Signar was afoot,
his mount dead behind him with a lance through its belly.
The Rhemians, though, were less than pleased with this small
victory. They had expected a single warrior their own size,
riding double, and were appalled to find a giant Vikonen in
their midst who cared not a whit whether he was on horse,
afoot or nesting in a tree. He had already dropped two of
these fellows with a terrible sweep of his war axe. His roar
thundered through the clearing and shook the earth. The four
remaining soldiers circled him warily, near as frightened as
their mounts, who wanted nothing to do with this horror.

The girl screamed. I swept her to the ground and plunged
into the fray. The closest Rhemian jerked about, startled to
find me there. His blade came up but there was no time for it.
He sank with a little cry and slid to earth. His horse took wing
and tore through heavy timber, showering dry leaves behind.

Signar had wounded another, putting him out of the fight.
The remaining pair learned quickly about Vikonens, and
stayed well out of his reach. He watched them, dark amusement in his eyes. He was playing with them now, lumbering
back and forth, flicking his great axe in their way like a small
boy poking at wasps. "Come, children, play with old Signar,"
he told them. "Bring your little stickers up close and I'll shave
them nice and clean."

I heard it, then, from the right—coming on fast. "Signar."

He couldn't hear, or wouldn't. The Vikonen do peculiar things to their heads in the heat of battle. While they are in this condition, they are far from normal beings.

"Signar! To me!" He gave me one eye. "They come, the others!" I pointed through the trees.

"Then come they must," he growled. "My mount is dead, Aldair, and I cannot ride these other beasts, which are little bigger than hares."

"You can, for a while."

He gave me a long and sober look. "Not long enough. You know this is so."

A chill climbed up my back. "Signar. We cannot stay here!"

"I can."

"You do me no honor in that."

"Aldair. What *you* do, must be done. Would you turn aside from the task—for your life or mine? Go, now!"

"Perhaps I would," I grinned, "if there was any place else to go. As you can see, there is not."

They came through the woods above, where the trees were no thicker than parkland, and they had picked up help along the way. I could not count them all. Suffice it to say, they were far more than we needed.

This is perhaps the best way—and the worst—to view a Rhemian line of battle. It is an awesome, and strangely beautiful sight. At a distance, these fellows are no longer the flat-snouted street toughs who swagger about our streets, making light of our ways and tracking southern mud across our honor. Their armor shines, even under dreary skies, and at a signal, pennoned lances dip at a deadly, practiced angle. At such moments, it is easy to see how they have taken the earth as their own.

It is a marvelous spectacle, but as I say, there are perhaps safer ways to see it. They were fair upon us, and little we could do to stop them. Signar and I looked at each other and said words that did not need the saying.

This was not, though, the end of our ventures. What happened, happened swiftly—in no more time than it takes to speak the words. It was a thing scarcely seen, and I recount it as best I can.

There came a howl that filled the forest hollow and chilled the blood. It was every northchild's nightmare come to life, and before it fell away, something fast and gray swept like a mist through the Rhemian ranks. It ripped and slashed and tore and left dark gouts of red behind. Three armored riders fell dead, and then another—and none but the last had time to see what killed him. Rhemian horse are trained to stay in battle, but not against the smell of Stygianns. This Lord of the Lauvectii knew he gave the scent of fear, and relished it. Before the riders brought themselves to order he ripped the bellies of another mount or two, and pulled a rider to the ground. Finally, they came down hard upon him, too many at a time, and he leaped into our clearing, ahead of their lances. The great sword of Albion was at his side, but he had not drawn it in this battle.

Signar moved without a word to let him in our circle. He had no love for Stygianns, but this was another matter. The Rhemians stopped short, not certain how they wished to handle this new arrangement. I took my place to Signar's right, the Stygiann beside me.

"It appears that you are ever in some forest where you don't belong," he told me.

"I could say the same, *Stygiaar,* unless I have misplaced the River Rheinus. Though I can't say I'm sorry to see you." Signar growled deep in his chest, but said nothing.

At a quick count, I made the Rhemians at fifteen. The pair Signar had backed against the forest had fled the field. We had honed their numbers nicely, but not enough.

"You make a good counting," I told the Stygiann, "but I fear we have merely prolonged a sorry ending."

"I would expect such words from the *char'desh,*" he sniffed. "For myself, I have no intention of dying in such company as yourself and this hairy mountain. That would be unseemly."

Signar cast a baleful eye over his shoulder. "It would be *seemly* if we could discuss this another time, over good barley beer. These fellows are growing restless."

I was wondering just how we might arrange this drinking bout, when a bit of color caught my eye. It was crawling about beneath the grasses, against the forest wall. I laughed aloud, rammed my sword to earth, and went after it. It saw me coming and gave a little cry, scampering away on bruised and pretty knees.

"Hold, lady, you may be useful yet!"

She wailed as I brought her to her feet, kicking and flailing about. The Rhemians saw her. Shouts of anger rose from their ranks, and for a moment, they surged in upon us. I stopped them quickly, holding the female before me with a dagger at her throat. "Soldiers," I called out, "how badly do you want us?"

One brought his mount a step forward. He was clearly the captain of this band—a good soldier, but most unhappy with his charge today. He watched me coldly, but said nothing.

"What's it to be, then?" I asked him.

"Let her go. You will not be harmed."

I laughed. "Sir, do not take me for a turnip. I don't know who I have here. But you do."

He tried to show me nothing, but his eyes betrayed him. "If you harm her—"

"If I harm her, she'll be of no value, will she? Now. Go back where you came from, and quickly. I am not fool enough to think you won't be in our tracks—but take a care that I don't see you there."

He sat a long moment, and many unkind thoughts found their way between us.

"I look forward to facing you again," he said stiffly. "It is a day that will give me great pleasure." With that, he granted me a short, contemptuous salute, and turned his mount away.

At the time, I am certain that neither of us truly believed he would fill this promise. Certainly, we could not have dreamed how such a day would come about.

FOUR

The sun was not yet over the land, but the day promised bright, clear skies with crisp winds from the north. I joined Signar at the little finger of stone that pushed out over the sea. He heard me there, but did not take his eyes from the chill gray waters.

"I do not see them," he told me, "but they will be here. There is still time upon the tide."

"I have no doubt of this. There is no better ship, or crew. The whole ungainly fleet of Rhemia could scarcely turn them back."

Signar turned to face me, bunching his great shoulders against the wind. "Aldair, we know there is a chance they saw us come ashore before. Certainly, they know the ship and will be watching for it. Now, there is more to feed their ire." He nodded toward the female, bound and bundled in the trees behind us. "I know it's in your thinking that she pays our passage from this place. But I tell you, friend, they will never let us have her. The Rhemians are no fools, and they well know she is lost forever, once we reach the sea."

I didn't answer. We had not seen them during long days and nights crossing near all of Gaullia to the sea. We knew, of course, that they were there. It is a wearing thing to know your enemy is just beyond your campfires in the night, and close upon your tracks throughout the day. It makes for poor sleeping and short tempers. We were all the worse for it, though I will say it was better than it could have been. That is, none of us had slain the other, which is something. Signar

23

would not speak to the Stygiann, and rumbled within his chest if that one even looked his way. The Stygiann, of course, found this amusing, which only added coals to the fire.

I will say nothing of the female, save that she was insufferable, and wholly dedicated to making us as miserable as possible. She would neither eat nor drink. She did not speak, or even show that we were alive. There was only one occasion when I got the best of her. She refused to walk, or ride her mount, and stated firmly that if she was to be kidnapped, I would have to carry her wherever we were going. I said that I would not, but that the Stygiann would be more than pleased to help her. There was no more trouble after that. She was terrified of him, and certain he intended to eat her before the trip was over. I am not too certain this was not upon his mind. All in all, I can remember more enjoyable times.

"There is a thing that I would ask," said Signar, pretending to watch the sea.

"I can guess what it is. The Stygiann?"

Signar mumbled to himself.

"To answer the question you have not yet asked—I cannot say, Signar. He has come this far, has he not?"

"He has not *said* he'll go further, though, has he?" I had to laugh at the hopeful tone in his voice. "Signar, we have seen much together. We are more than comrades for we share a terrible secret between us, a thing that binds the threads of our lives." I stopped, reached out and touched his arm. "Knowing that secret as you do, and what it means, do you not wonder that things may—happen, that neither of us fully comprehend? I cannot say about the Stygiann. I know only that I *had* to cross the River Rheinus, and do what I did."

He gave me a distant, curious look. "At the woods. You knew he'd be there. It was a thing that I could see . . ."

"No." I shook my head. "I did not. I cannot explain what I know and what I do not. This is a thing you have ever found difficult to comprehend, old friend. I am neither seer nor wise man, but only what you see. I do not know where this task will take us, any more than you do. For the most part, I am a chip floating upon the sea, with no direction. Direction is there, but it is seldom clearly seen. If it was," I grinned, "would I wander about like a radish, and act the fool as I do? Creator knows, I would not!"

Signar shook his head and ran a big hand past his muzzle. "I don't know," he said wearily, "it's plain to me I'm a far better captain of ships than I am a thinker, and I'm glad enough to leave that part of our ventures to you."

"We are in dire need of help, then," I said soberly, "if I'm the full weight of our wisdom."

I found the Stygiann to the rear of our camp, well in the midst of a stand of trees. And though I knew he was there, and could clearly see his gaunt gray form and murder-red eyes, he was still no more than shadow out of shadow.

"Do you see them?"

"No," he said, "but they are there. And more have arrived of late. They must be pleased to find you have backed yourself against water with no place to go."

A Stygiann is ever the same. They hear what they wish to, and easily ignore the rest. "I have explained before what we are about. We *do* have a place to go. Our ship is coming on the tide to take us away. It is a fine ship, named after your kinsman. *Ahzir al'Rhaz* means Far Wanderer from the North."

He opened his jaws and stared. "And you call *that* a place to go?" His nose wrinkled in disgust. "I would as soon stick dung in my ears."

"Then you do not plan to go with us."

"What? Of course not! A Stygiann does not cross great pieces of water. There is not point to it. Besides, it would be most unseemly."

"Your kinsman Rheif crossed a great many *pieces* of water," I pointed out.

"So you say. Though I did not see this, and can scarce believe it. I do note, however, that Rheif and his brothers are all dead—which says something about Stygianns and their dealings with water."

"Then you will go back to the Lauvectii?"

"Indeed. I should never have left in the first place."

"And why did you?"

He glared at me. "You ask a great many questions, *char'-desh*."

"There are a great many things that need answering. How you happened to be in the woods outside Duroctium, for instance."

"That is my concern, not yours."

"You weren't looking for me, though."

"You?" He made a face. "And the fat mountain? Of course not."

"Fine." I stood, and looked up at him. "We have had little

time to talk upon this journey, *Stygiaar*. Evidently, there is little we have to say to one another. Though I would thank you for what you have done. Whatever the reason."

"I cannot accept your thanks. It would be unseemly to do so."

"It was *seemly* enough to take the sword I gave you—after you assured me it was not a gift you cared for. I see you do not scorn to *wear* it, for all your lofty talk!"

He stared at me with those terrible red eyes, but I did not look away. It was he who turned and stalked from me, snapping a small twig from a tree and thrusting it in his mouth. "There is a thing I would say," he told me, still not facing my way. "Though I cannot truly understand why I must say it. It may be that I have taken leave of my senses. After you left the Lauvechtii, I looked upon the weapon. Not because I cared to—I was duty bound to see if it was some trick of the *char'desh* to plague the *Stygiaar*. I saw the thing upon its hilt. The head of some beast, patterned in gold. I looked upon it but once, then covered it from sight, for it did not appear to be a seemly thing."

He paused a long moment. "That night I had a god-dream. In the dream was Rheif. He was in a far place, and death was upon him. And this is a most peculiar thing. It *was* a far place, yet it was not."

"You are right in both respects," I told him quietly. "Rheif died there, just across these waters on Island Albion. It is near, and its white shores can be seen on a cloudless day. Yet, it is a place that is strangely apart from all others."

The Stygiann jerked around, his red eyes wide with the only hint of fear I ever saw there. "This cannot be," he said darkly. "We know that place. It is the isle of your dead, and if you buried Rheif there as you say you are a specter yourself— either that, or you have lied to me!"

"I am very much alive," I assured him, "and I did not lie, Stygiann. But I can say no more on this."

He held my gaze a long moment. Anger was still in him, but it was no longer a killing thing. "In this god-dream," he said, "Rheif became as another. For an instant, he was a Stygiann no more. He was the beast upon the hilt of this sword! And this is why I left the woods of the Lauvectii. I am sorely troubled by this dream, and would know what it means. Now, you have put this dead place into my mind, and my thoughts are darker still."

Something knowing touched me, and was gone.

*You are the one, then Stygiann. I know your name, but I
would have you speak it to me. For it is you, truly, that I
sought in the dark of the Lauvectii!*

Whatever held him, let him go. The red fires died behind
his eyes. "I have been thinking," he said suddenly, "it may be
that I will walk upon this boat of yours. Just to see how it feels.
As you say, it bears the name of my kinsman—though I cannot see how a thing which floats upon the water could honor
itself with the name of a Stygiann."

"You would be welcome," I told him.

"You understand, of course, that I have no intention of going a'venturing on such a thing."

"Yes, I understand. It would probably not be seemly."

When the sun turned the sea to chilly gold, and quick winds
caught the sails of the *Ahzir*, I saw him standing there on the
headland, where we ourselves had stood only moments before.
It is hard to tell one Rhemian from another at such a distance, but I could see his tight, troubled brows and searching
eyes as easily as if he were next to me.

There were troops at his call, but he did not try to stop us.
There were warships he might have summoned. But he did not.

I could read his thinking as if it was my own. She would
die if he tried to take her. Or so he believed. Perhaps we would
kill her away. If she *could* live, though—whatever the cost—
she must be given that chance. Not for the first time, I wondered just what sort of prize I had taken from the streets of
Duroctium?

FIVE

With good winds, it is only a short journey south from the Gaullian coast to the narrow straits of the Southern Sea. In truth, though, this is not a trip that can be measured in days, for these two climes might well be world apart. Those of us who call the drear skies and dark forests of the Northland home do not really know the sun. To us, it is an occasional, welcome guest. Here, in the south, is where it was born.

I was as glad as Signar-Haldring to be at sea again, though all aboard did not appear to share this feeling. Our Stygiann friend complained constantly that the *Ahzir* was both too small and too fast, and though he knew next to nothing about sailing, swore our craft was unseaworthy.

"If Stygianns built ships," he declared, "which they would not, they would make sure the vessels did not rock back and forth in the water. I cannot imagine why no one has thought of this before." Signar immediately banned him from the bridge, and rightly so.

On the morning of our second day at sea, the Vikonen called me forward to see what awaited us. He was clearly less than pleased. "There, you see?" He pointed, though it was not necessary to give directions. We were passing the port city which I knew was called Camelium. It is a beautiful town, with bright houses climbing the green hills above the sea. It is a fishing town, as well as a trading center, and we sailed quite near the fleet of stubby little boats that bob about like colored corks upon the water.

This, however, was not the sight that held my eyes. Four

Rhemian warships loomed ahead, high decks topped with armored turrets above a triple row of oars. Banners snapped in the morning wind, and blood-red sails stood at the ready.

"It is clear we have not been forgotten," Signar said glumly. "It's the female, of course."

I didn't answer. We both knew what had happened. The Rhemians had sent fast messengers overland to alert their vessels down the coast. Not too surprising, as the girl was clearly of value to someone.

"They will hound us to death, Aldair, as long as she's aboard. There's no getting around it."

"And if we let her go? What then, Signar? No, they'll bite our heels if we keep her—but they'd swallow us whole if we didn't."

"Maybe," he said darkly. For a moment, he stared out over the water, big shoulders huddled in thought. "It's yours to decide, but if it was me I'd raise a good sail and set her adrift behind. We'd lose 'em sure while they put about, and they'd never catch us in those great ungainly tubs." He paused, and gave me a meaningful look. "It's a chance, but one worth taking. Do you truly want them forever in our wake, with what we're about?"

Of course, I did not, and told him so.

"Well, then . . ."

"You forget, there's more than one set of those tubs afloat. The Straits belong to Rhemia, and we won't have Niceans to guard our flanks this time."

He admitted this was so, and reluctantly agreed the female was needed for a time. After we safely passed the Rhemian fortress, into the Southern Sea, I promised we would think again on the matter. Though I knew I would feel the same about it then. If the truth be known, I did not want to see her go.

To dissuade the Rhemian vessels, I had the girl brought topside and perched her in the bow under guard. She was in full view, and clearly alive. The crewmen at her side were warned again that she was not to be trusted. It would not have surprised me in the least if she had decided to dive into the sea, and swim to her friends.

The Rhemians were plainly waiting for her to appear, for one of their great warships moved in quickly for a look. It was a testy moment. This monstrous hulk loomed above our decks, churning enough water to swamp a lesser craft. The soldiers in her turrets could near spit upon our sails, and I suppose some tried. Signar roared and cursed them all, and shook his great fist at the captain. Then, he showed them why Vikonens are the finest sailors in the world . . .

While we were yet in the shadow of this craft, he put our crew to life and brought the *Ahzir al'Rhaz* about smoothly, near standing her on her side in the water. For a moment, the sleek vessel creaked and shuddered in protest. We held onto whatever was handy while the hull veered sharply over, and watched blue water coming up to meet us. Then, just as I was certain we'd never right ourselves in time, the ship leaped out ahead of the wind like a hare, and left the Rhemians behind.

I could hear Signar's great, booming laughter, even above the shriek of the wind. Try *that* in your fine floating chamber pot, he was saying—and though none aboard the other vessel heard him, I'm certain her captain got the message.

I had to grin at the Stygiann. His pointed ears were flat against his skull, and all the color had left his eyes. Like all of us, he was soaked to the skin with salt water. His fine fur pelt looked all the world like old gray rags that had scrubbed too many floors.

"It is easy for you to laugh," he said darkly. "I would not be surprised if that great barrel of ale did that intentionally. He would sink us, to make me look foolish."

"Stygiaar," I said, "whatever you may think of the Vikonen, I will tell you that you have just witnessed a masterful piece of seamanship. It is a thing to tell your kinsmen, when you return to the Lauvectii."

He muttered to himself and rubbed water from his ears. "It will not be necessary to collect tales of this voyage," he said gloomily, "for I can see already I will never return to the north. Which serves me right, I suppose. I should never have allowed you to trick me into stepping onto these floors in the first place."

"Decks. Not floors," I corrected. "And not even a Stygiann, who is a master of lies, can hope to make me believe he did not come aboard this ship of his own free will. Creator's Eyes —you probably believe this tale yourself!"

The Stygiann sniffed and looked away. "It is not seemly for a Lord of the Lauvectii to argue with *char'desh*. I see no point in this."

"In that, I would agree."

"The fact is, I am certain I will drown in this pond that has no ending. The Lauvectii know these things, though it would not be seemly to explain how this is done. For this reason, I wish my name to be known to you. For though you are not of my people, and have no honor, you should be able to announce my coming to the wood-gods. If they will listen to voices that come off the water, which I doubt. At any rate, when the time comes, you will please remember that I am Rhalgorn."

With that, he made his way below, trying valiantly to look like a warrior, instead of a hare that has lately hopped out of a stew. Thus, I learned my new companion's name, which was somehow already in my mind. And he, in turn, satisfied his pride by choosing this bizarre manner of introducing himself.

The Rhemians did not try to catch us again, but were content to keep us in sight. Even this seemed to challenge their powers. Signar is right. Rhemians truly hate the sea, and use it only because they have to. This is reflected in the way they build their ships, which more resemble overturned shops and stables than anything meant to catch the wind. Certainly, they are nothing like the slim green craft of the Niceans, which seem born of the foam, or the fast, high-prowed ships of the Vikonen that sweep down from Vhiborg to raid the Rhemian ports. The *Ahzir*, of course, is something of both, bringing the best of the two together. And I do not believe there is anything afloat that can match her.

The Rhemians knew this, too, and were well aware they would be hard pressed to keep us in sight if we chose to lose them. Thus, when we rounded the bulge of the Tarconii peninsula next morning, I was not surprised to find the big ships out of sight, and another on hand to take their places. This was a ship of the Niceans, which had somehow fallen into Rhemian hands. It was a good ship, with beautiful lines—it could not overtake us easily, but we would find it equally as hard to leave it behind.

"They will not let you go, you know. You are a fool to try to keep me here."

I turned, surprised and pleased to find her there, and nodded her guard away. "It is good of you to join us," I told her. "Your friends will want to see you looking well."

She shrugged carelessly, to let me know she had not come up for that, but for reasons of her own. Her fine satin gown had been tattered and soiled on our trek across Gaullia, and she was now adorned in seaman's clothes, garments hardly designed to fit her form. Still, I thought her the most beautiful creature I had ever seen. Just to be in her presence did peculiar things to me. I'm sure she was aware of this.

"Though I do not wish to speak to you, I find that I must," she said. "I demand to know what you intend to do with me."

I raised a brow at that. *"Demand,* lady? You forget. The boot of Rhemia is that way." I nodded toward the east.

She studied me a long moment with no expression at all. "What kind of person *are* you? Though we come from different stations, our people are the same. Yet, you sail with Vikonen, who are nothing more than pirates. And worse, you consort with—Stygianns." Her mouth twisted, as if it hurt to say the word. "That horrible creature! His brothers prey upon your lands and slaughter your kin. Yet, you fight beside him against Rhemian soldiers." She shuddered, and looked away. "I do not see how this can be. What *are* you?"

"Lady," I told her, "I am a person who has learned that the shape of a creature has little to do with his heart. I have been betrayed by my own kind—including Good Fathers of the Church and fine citizens of Rhemia. I have found both friends and enemies among the Niceans, who are green and scaled and far stranger than Stygianns. There is both good and bad in every race I have encountered, and I haven't noticed that one appears to cheat at dice, or murder with more frequency, than another."

"And so you have all banded together," she said contemptuously, "to kidnap Rhemian females and carry them off. Is this your highest pursuit in life, then?"

"No, There is another."

She laughed. "I am sure I would love to hear it."

"And I am just as sure that you would not."

Her face went deadly pale, then, and she touched her throat with the tips of her fingers. "Please—you must not do this thing."

"You are most difficult to let go, Lady. Or keep, for that matter. It seems we are damned either way we leap. Maybe I'd find it easier to decide upon a proper path if I knew who it was we were kidnapping, and why the entire Rhemian navy wants her back. You are a most attractive female, I admit—but I have a feeling there's more to it than that."

She flushed angrily, and her eyes made tiny points. "It may be you will discover who I am, sooner than you think. To your own great sorrow!"

On that cryptic note, she turned and stalked away, leaving me with a last haughty flick of her pretty pink snout.

The ship stayed in our wake until the sun was well behind us both. Signar had timed us well since the morning, and we would pass through the Straits by night. This did not entirely solve the problem of our follower, but I was certain we could lose him eventually. We did—but not in the manner I had hoped for. . . .

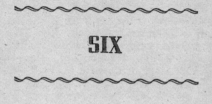

SIX

Usually, when there is a storm at sea, a sailor has some warning of its coming. There are signs upon the water and in the winds which the seafarer can read as easily as a scholar scans his books. I have known Signar to look at a clear, bright sky and announce that we were in for a dismal display of weather.

The storm that raged down upon us in the first hour of the night followed none of the rules of the sea, for this great wind was born of the land. It hugged the low hills of the Tarconii peninsula, hauling cold scudding clouds in its wake, then struck without warning. We could not reach the coast for shelter, or follow our course to the Straits. We clung to what we could, and even bound ourselves to masts and timbers— for the sea was dark and angry, and hungry for us all.

By dawn, the great ocean was flat and green as a farm pond, with hardly a ripple on its surface. Shortly before, there had been more wind than one could ask for in a lifetime—now, there was scarcely enough breeze to keep a gnat aloft. Signar growled, and frowned at our empty sails.

"I hope you're up to some good arm-wrenching exercises," he said. "We're in for a day's rowing, 'less that sky does some fancy changing."

"At any rate," I told him, "we've left our pursuers far behind. If they haven't sunk themselves, they may decide that we have." It was a logical premise, though neither of us believed the Rhemians would be satisfied with anything less than great pieces of the *Ahzir* floating about. They are a perverse and stubborn people. Once, it is said, half the Empire was lost while some tyrant of the moment dispersed his legions in quest of a mouse with golden eyes. If this is true, our followers would not be dissuaded from a prize far more tangible than a mythical rodent.

As near as Signar could tell, we were well to the south and west of the coast of Kenyarsha, which is the name given that great mass of land below the Southern Sea. A crewman who had served on a Rhemian trader claimed there was a port called Bhazaar, somewhere below the Straits, which belonged to the Rhemians—though of course he had never been there.

I was somewhat leery of this, for though we had the best Niciean charts available, I could find no such city. Indeed, the map itself ended just below the Straits. Kenyarsha is clearly a great land, but little is known about it. The Nicieans lived around its northern shores, but seldom travel inland, except to trade or fight with the desert folk.

Nevertheless, we had little choice in the matter, unless we cared to sail south into waters we didn't know, or west, where it is said the Misty Sea falls off into nothing.

Since mine is a free ship, each crewman took his turn at the oars—even Rhalgorn, though Stygianns abhor work of any kind. At midday, a pleasant wind came up, and made our labors easier. And soon after that, fortune came our way. The lookout sighted land, a dark green line on the eastern horizon. This was news that brought us cheering from our benches—though I was not as happy at this sight as I might have been. Our knowledge of Niciea was more than two years old, now. We had left a shattered empire behind, its king in flight. If that most unholy alliance between Fhazir and the priests of Aastar was still in power, friends of the royal family would not be welcome on those shores.

"It does not overly matter," said Signar, when I shared my concern on this. "I did not wish to speak of it before, as there were greater problems at hand. We will have to make land somewhere; there is salt from the storm in both our food and water casks."

"It is a fine way to begin a venture," I complained. "We are not yet through the Straits, having left them far behind. When we *get* there, more Rhemian friends will be on hand to greet us. I do not like this, Signar. Our task is not for the world to see. We must be rid of these fellows, and soon!"

Signar nodded without speaking. When he is chewing on a problem of some sort, he rocks back and forth in a kind of silent dance, to music only he can hear. At such times, there is little use in talking.

In spite of the possibility of an unfriendly welcome, my heart sang out at the sight of the small white city off our bow. It could not rival Chaarduz, but it was distinctly Niciean, and I warmed to it at once. I have been both a slave, and a person of high honors in this land, and I greatly love its people.

A crewman with sharper eyes than mine gave a shout, and I followed his gaze to shore. We were indeed in luck— for the green pennon bright with golden eyes still flew over the city! As we watched, slim green forms in hooded robes lined the quayside and waved in our direction. Clearly, they knew our vessel, and in their honor I raised the Niciean flag to our mast, and beneath it, the personal pennant of the Aghiir, Lord Tharrin, who was brother to the king. This gesture brought such cheers and shouting from the crowd I thought they would all take to water—though Nicieans do not get wet if they can help it. Instead, many sleek green sailing craft took to sea, and came swiftly out to meet us.

First among these was a small boat bearing a seemingly berserk creature in its bow. He yelled and waved and hopped about in a most un-Niciean manner. As the craft grew closer, I decided the sun had surely damaged my eyes. Nicieans look very much alike unless you know them. Their faces, to us, lack true features, for they have bright, lidless eyes, and only slits and gashes where a nose and mouth should be. I knew every shiny scale on this creature, though— for his name was Thareesh, and he was perhaps the finest archer in the world, after me. It seemed most unlikely that he was sailing toward me in a small boat, and thrashing his tail about, for I had left him for dead in the Great Desert below Chaarduz, more than three full years before!

SEVEN

No doubt, many would think this happy reunion a most peculiar sight. We have fought Niceans since the beginning of time—or so the priests of both our races would have you believe. Nevertheless, we greeted one another like brothers—for so we have ever seemed to be.

I was thirsty for news of Niciea and Thareesh was water from the well. First, though, I insisted upon hearing his own adventures at least twice—how he had been captured by rebels more dead than alive, become one of them for a time to save himself, and finally made his escape across the whole of Niciea to this port.

The king, he said, was dead for certain, and much of the royal family and its followers. There were many new names to toast. But there was good news as well. The promises of Fhazir and the priests had come to nothing, and the people were restless and angry. They had already forgotten their own folly had brought disaster on their heads.

"The traitors' days are numbered," Thareesh said darkly. "There are many places such as this, where old banners fly. And it is not just the rich and the rabble who come," he added hastily. "There are soldiers like myself a'gathering—here, and everywhere."

"And who do they follow," I asked him, "with the king and his brother both dead?"

"Why, the young *Dhar' jeem,* of course. You, of all people, Aldair, should know that this is so."

A Nicean does not betray his thoughts, unless he wishes

to. I did not think he could have known that it was I who carried the infant prince to safety in the east. If he did, though, I was not concerned. Niciea has no more loyal subject than Thareesh.

While no words passed between us on the matter, Thareesh immediately busied himself with the provisioning of the *Ahzir,* haggling with merchants and traders for the best goods and prices. Signar, of course, was delighted. By evening, there were three other Niceans aboard, all experienced seaman, and welcome additions to the crew.

Somehow, I had known from the beginning that Thareesh would join us, too. Rhalgorn, for Rheif. And now a Nicean in our circle, a fierce and loyal follower of my own dead friend and master. Wherever the Lord Tharrin might be, I knew that he would smile upon this choice. It seemed, that night, as if the stars had come together in their courses. That the time, indeed, was right for new beginnings. I *knew* that it was so.

This is not always the way, by any means. I know that I am guided in some manner, but I can rarely say just when and where. I am certainly under no illusion that Great Powers guard my belly from the thrust of a short sword. It may be this has happened, for I have been whisper-close to death more than once. But who'd be fool enough to guess just when his lucky time might come again?

At any rate, I know there was a magic in that evening, a thing I could not put away. It lingered there, and made itself known to us all. Light from bronze and silver lamps splashed the dark timbers with gold, and in a trick of shadows I could imagine it was the old Aghiir himself who sat there, and not Thareesh. Rhalgorn, gray and brooding, could well have been his kinsman Rheif. There was no imagining Signar, his great fist hard around a tankard of ale. And I am certain by the look in his black-agate eyes that he, too, was taken by the moment. The spell was upon us, and it was neither now nor yesteryear, but some dusty hour in between. . . .

Signar and I had spoken earlier to Thareesh of our pursuit by Rhemians, and now it crossed my mind that he would not easily understand how our captive Lady could cause such havoc, as females play a somewhat different role in Niciea. Nevertheless, he said nothing about this.

"I do not think they will pursue you here," he said. "But

that does not mean they could not, if they wished." He looked up at that, his lidless eyes on mine. "In the old days, they would not have dared the sea lanes of Niciea. Now . . ."

"And what of the Southern Sea," I asked him. "Could a single ship go undetected there?"

"Undetected? I do not think so, Aldair. They are slow and ungainly, these Rhemians, but they are thick as flies, and there is nothing left to stand in their way."

Signar drained his ale and watched me over the rim of his mug. You see? his eyes told me, it is just as I said.

"At any rate," I spoke aloud, "it is there we must go, Thareesh."

"The Niciean has told you how it will be," said Signar.

"We are faster than anything they can muster. Even the few Niciean vessels in their hands cannot outsail the *Ahzir*."

"They cannot," growled the Vikonen, slamming his tankard down heavily on our table, "unless we have bad winds, lose our sails, run aground—any of a hundred things that can befall even the best of captains. Which I do not mind admitting, is myself. Such hazards alone do not promise disaster, Aldair. One can expect a fair amount of trouble at sea. But with Rhemians on our tail, can we truly—" He caught himself, looked quickly at Rhalgorn and Thareesh, then stared at me with great alarm.

"—risk what we have at stake?" I finished for him. "It's all right to say it now, old friend. These are our companions —they are here because they should be here, and they must know what we're about."

Thareesh didn't move. Rhalgorn lifted his muzzle from a haunch of meat and licked his teeth. I met their eyes, but said nothing for a moment.

And then I told them. . .

I told it as well as I could, beginning at the beginning. How I fled the University at Silium, accused of crimes I had not committed. How Rheif and I escaped together in a small boat, glimpsing the dread shores of Albion through the mist. I did not need to tell them of Albion Isle, for though neither the Stygianns nor Niciceans share the beliefs of the Church, they know that awesome place. To the Lords of the Lauvectii, it is a nightmare land, where dream-things dwell. To the Niciceans, who live in the warmth of the southern sun, it is a damp and barren hell. For my people, it is the Dark Isle, where the souls of the dead roam about forever.

Only, I have been to Island Albion, and it is none of these things. There is death there, of a sort—but it is not the death of the Afterworld. There is shame, sorrow and dishonor. And worse than these.

I told how we drifted south, to be captured and enslaved by the Lord Tharrin. It was he who taught me the love of old cities, and made me his aide at that ancient site on Tarconii. And it was he who shared with me the beginnings of a secret that would one day take him to his death, and help bring all Niciea down in ruin.

Like all good sons of the Church in my own land, I believed what I was taught, that history began three-thousand years ago, with the Creation. Beyond that, was the Darkness. Lord Tharrin showed me the folly in this: *some sort of being had walked the streets of that dead Tarconii city some five-thousand years before the fabled Darkness of the Church!*

There was more—much more, as I came to learn. Tharrin was not the fount of this knowledge, but only a link. A Cygnian slave who was not a slave was his master in these teachings. And again, his master was another—a being who lives in a powder-musty place in the Great Desert to the east, a seer with fur sleek as water and satin, and yellow-green eyes set on end like pumpkin seeds. It was he, then, who set me on the quest that brought me at last to Island Albion.

I have said I told the story as well as I could. But how can one speak of the Dark Isle, so that those who hear it understand? I told of massive oaks, thick as columns . . . the game that abounds there where no arrow has found its mark in countless years. I told of the white bones of a great dead city—pale, spectral fingers that thrust beyond the crowns of the highest trees.

Finally, I told how I made my way beneath that city, and discovered the secret of Albion. . .

. . .Doors of polished metal, that open with a whisper . . . lights that burn cold and steady, like no lamps in the world. . . .

There were a thousand ghost-gray windows that move and speak, and picture what has gone before. I watched these windows come to life as I stood before them, and saw history as it happened. There were beings like myself, who lived by the sea in earthen huts. The huts became villages, the villages cities, the cities small kingdoms. I watched the founding of the Rhemian Empire . . . the beginnings of the Niceans and Vikonens . . . the migration of Stygianns from the east . . . the enslavement of the Cygnians . . . I saw creatures that fly, and live in great towers, and creatures that live beneath the sea. . . . Some of the gray windows did not come to life, and I cannot guess what stories they told.

Somewhere in that great and hollow place I came upon the first pictures of the things with no hair. Even a Cygnian whose wool has been freshly shorn was never so bare and ugly. They had little blobs for snouts, wide red slits for mouths, and ears like baby mice.

It was they, I learned, who had built the city, and others like it—cities that towered to the skies. They strode about these wondrous places like kings, soared above the land like tiny bees in a bubble. And on a day in some dread summer, long ago, I saw them make the world. . . .

I saw creatures like myself brought from shiny cases and set naked on a hill. I saw them cling to each other, and cry out in fear. I saw this happen to Vikonens, and Niceans, and the rest. Only these are names the hairless creatures gave us. They are not the names of what we are. I know those names, but I will not say them—for I have seen the things we were before we were changed, and sent naked into the world. I have seen the glass cages, and the things within, frozen with the look of life. . . A shaggy giant on four legs, sweeping a fish from the water. . . .a gaunt gray creature howling at the moon. . .a crawling thing with emerald hide, basking in the sun. . . .a woolly beast with heavy fleece and placid eyes. . .

I have seen myself, too. A fat little creature with hooves and a curly tail. I was eating dried corn beside a fence. There was a female nearby, suckling her young. . . .

And that is the terrible secret of Island Albion. We are not men of different races, as we thought ourselves. We are not men at all, but made things, given hands and feet instead of hooves and paws. Set in motion like silly toys to mock or amuse our makers.

And why? So that Men could become as gods? Or less than that—to show some great and terrible hate for themselves?

There was no sound in the cabin of the *Ahzir*, only the
faint creak of timber, and the lapping of the sea. Neither
Rhalgorn nor Thareesh could find words. Indeed, what
words would suffice for a creature who has found that he is
not a man at all, but a thing given speech by another?

"That is only the beginning of the sin of Man," I told
them. "He was not content to make us, and set us on the
Earth to live our lives. He has made us after himself—a
mockery of Man, to follow in his steps."

Rhalgorn looked up. He was nearly ashen under his fur,
but there was cold anger in his eyes. "Aldair, one can lock
a hare in a cage, but he cannot turn it into a bird."

"This is indeed what Aldair is trying to tell you," blurted
Signar. "Birds we are, whether we like it or not!"

Rhalgorn would speak again, but I stopped him. "This
is the greater sin I speak of, Stygiann. We *cannot* live our
own lives, as free creatures. I have seen the histories of Man
in that place. Not all of them, for certain, but enough to
know. There were creatures like yourself among Men, who
lived in the Northern woods and harried my people. There
was an empire like that of the Rhemians, who sought to
conquer the world." I looked at Signar and Thareesh. "And
Northmen, in their longboats. Desert folk, who ruled the
coast of the Southern Sea. *We are repeating that history,
Rhalgorn. We are chained to his victories and his defeats—
he has stamped his own destiny upon our souls!*"

For the first time, the Niciean spoke. "May Aastar curse
him, and his children!" he spat. Then, sadly, with a shrug,
"if indeed there is a Creator beyond Man to do the cursing.
I never imagined I would utter such heresy, but I have said
it."

Rhalgorn threw back his head and laughed. It was not a
sound we expected, and it took us all aback. "Niciean," he
said, "I know nothing of your gods, or their powers, but it
may be that yours, or mine or someone's has done the job
nicely. This *Man* is no longer with us, or his children."

"You are right in that," I said. "He is clearly no longer
about—but his curse is still upon us."

"Curses can be broken," Rhalgorn said soberly. He gripped
the hilt of his sword to show us how. "I have broken a few,
and may break another."

I looked at him, and then let my gaze rest upon the others.
Of a sudden, I felt an awesome surge of power flow between
us, and knew it was a thing far greater than the sum of the

four of us. There was something else there. It came briefly into the light, touched us, and was gone. But what it left behind was richer, and more complete, than we had known before.

Signar poured ale all around, with an extra measure for Rhalgorn and Thareesh, who had much to drown in their cups that night. We would have willingly joined them in this, but as it happened, not a drop of good barley found our lips. At that moment, the watch cried out and beat with a great clamor upon our door.

EIGHT

"What do you *mean*, gone?" Signar roared, lifting the frightened seaman off his feet, "gone *where*, damn you!"

Running boots and calls of alarm sounded from the decks. I pushed past the Vikonen and raced topside. L'siir, one of Thareesh's new crewmen, stopped me at the quarterdeck. "There, sir," he hissed, "to sea—" I followed his slim green hand, but saw nothing in the dark.

Rhalgorn spoke beside me. "It's well you have a Stygiann to do your looking, Aldair, else—"

"Just tell me what you see."

"It's the female, all right. She's a'sail in one of the little Niciean boats—the kind that looks like a pointy log with a bedsheet at its top."

The Niciean gave him a blood-look. Signar thundered up behind us. "There's worse yet, I fear. She bloodied the head of a guard somehow, and it was he who sounded the alarm." His short furry ears went flat against his skull. "The thing is, he remembers hearin' watch called just before she skinned him."

I stared, then understood. A chill started up my neck.

"Aye," Signar nodded. "She's been about near an hour or more, for certain."

"She heard, then. There's nothing else for it. We *have* to get her, friend. There are things she knows that must not leave her lips!"

Signar jerked a thumb over his shoulder. "We're under-

44

way, or will be. She'll not get far—unless we lose her in the dark."

I gripped his arm. "That must not happen!"

"Who would guess a female to have knowledge of sailing?" Thareesh said wondrously. I had not seen the archer come up, but one seldom hears a Niciean, as they are near as silent as Stygianns. "Is this a custom in your land, Aldair? I would guess that it is not."

"She doesn't know *much* about it," answered Signar. "She's heading south, with a good strong wind behind her, which seems the thing to do if you're a beginner at the mast. We'll be on her soon enough, and she'll not find her Rhemian friends in that direction."

Signar spoke too soon, however. Almost on his words the lookout shouted and sent our eyes to west-northwest, just above the horizon. Four dark sails came at us full sweep upon the night—three of the big square-sheeted Rhemians, and the captured Nicean we'd seen before. This last vessel was well ahead of the rest, prow slicing water like a fine blade. Signar cursed and bellowed orders. Our canvas shifted and rose, and we fair lifted off the water.

Moments later, a seaman called again, and we turned to watch Rhemian missiles arc across the night. There were a dozen or so, tiny grains of pea-sized fire that grew to great flaming suns, half as big as a farmer's cottage. Geysers rose in an even line to starboard. We were well out of range, and the Rhemians knew this. For the moment, they were merely taking our measure.

Rhalgorn gripped the rail beside me. "This is a fine venture you've gotten me into, Aldair. First you set my hairs on end with tales of dead souls and men who are not true men at all—then you set us helpless on the sea where *those* devils can have a good go at us. I do not like this, and I would like you to return me to the woods of the Lauvectii as soon as possible."

"I would happily join you there," I told him, "but I do not see how this can be accomplished at the moment."

The Rhemians heaved another volley our way, and then another. Neither was much closer than the first. We soon pulled well away, and they made no further efforts. One such missile amidships, of course, would see the end of us—but this would never happen unless we dropped our sail and waited like turnips or the kill. This was not the greatest of our worries, for certain. The big ungainly tubs were no better than grounded birds against us. We could outsail them several times over, barring troubles of our own.

The captured Niciean was something else again. It could keep us in sight, waiting for our luck to change. And this is a thing that happens to every sailor, sooner or later.

"We could turn and sail right through 'em in the dark, you know," Signar suggested hopefully. "I can cut that wind with ease and be away to the north."

"You know we have to find her, friend.'"

"We have to *see* her, first," he muttered, squinting into the dark.

"We have night eyes watching," I reminded him. "I doubt there's a Stygiann aboard the Rhemian craft. We have it on them, there."

"As that braggart lets me know twice a minute," said the Vikonen. He mouthed a curse in the direction of our bow. "Creator's Eyes, Aldair—the fellow's not to be believed!" I laughed over the wind. "He's another Rheif, for sure. All Stygianns are the same."

"Well, now. I wouldn't say that. Rheif was a fine friend, though given to some exaggeration. This one, now, is something else again."

A Stygiann grows upon a person, but the attachment is somewhat like a wart or errant hair: it is a condition that takes some getting used to.

He clung for dear life to the very beak of our vessel, which was shaped like the slim body of a dolphin. He was soaked and matted clear through with spray, and looked all the world like a leech on a log.

"Rhalgorn, you are a sorry sight indeed," I called out, edging my way up to him.

"It is most unseemly of you to say so," he mumbled. He took care not to open his jaws, but kept them firmly clamped against the sea. "Particularly since it is my sight that is wholly responsible for the safety of every creature aboard this boat."

"Ship. It is a ship, not a boat. And you are greatly appreciated."

"I doubt it. Stygianns are never truly esteemed by other races, and the world goes poorer for its ignorance."

I didn't argue this. It was not the proper time for it. "Do you see anything? Anything at all?"

"I am asked this every second or so. The answer, Aldair, is yes, I see something. I see a great many things, and all of them are called water."

My stomach fell at that. "You've *lost* her?"

"I didn't say that. I cannot see her—as a female creature in a boat, that is. It is difficult to explain. She is there, ahead, but she is merely a different shade of darkness, now."

I thought this quite an admission for a Stygiann. Rheif used to swear he could count the lice on a circling hawk, when I could not even see the hawk itself. "Do the best you can," I told him. "She must not tell her story to the Rhemians, Rhalgorn."

"Why?" he said wryly, not taking his eyes off the sea. "They would likely not believe it. I am certainly not sure that I do."

This was not true, of course. I had seen his face there in the cabin.

At an hour past midnight Rhalgorn sent word that through no fault of his own, he had lost the girl from sight. He still peered stubbornly into the darkness, but it was clear he did not expect to find anything.

"What was her heading," asked Signar, "when last you saw her?"

Rhalgorn looked at him blankly. "Heading? What is this heading, fat-fur? I am no sailor, full of mystic sea words."

Signar swallowed his thoughts. "Was she still going south? Turning north, or west?"

"East," grinned Rhalgorn. "South, a bit, but more than a hair to the east."

Signar and I looked at each other. "Toward the *land?*"

"Not of her own will, I'd imagine," said the Vikonen. "Wind and tide'll suck a small boat ashore sometimes, if you don't know your craft. And I figure she doesn't."

Signar was against it, but we set our course to port. I couldn't blame him for his caution. We knew nothing of the land here, or the depths offshore. The lookout aft reported that our follower had made the change in course right along with us, trailing dutifully in our wake. It was almost as if a stout line held us together.

We were so close to shore that we could see the dark mass of land to port. Thre was no shoreline to speak of, only a narrow white beach with a pale rise of combers. We dared not speak, for Signar had posted himself and his two best seamen in the prow with throwing cords to test the depths. Thus, we cut through black water in such silence we could hear the birds call out ashore. There were no stars to be seen, but I guessed the hour at three, or later.

And when the sun comes up, and we've yet to find her, I asked myself. What then? Perhaps, even now, she has somehow passed us, and is telling her tale to a Rhemian captain.

This, to me, was more perilous than I dared imagine. I did not share Rhalgorn's hope that the story would be easily dismissed. The Nicean priests of Chaarduz had gained but a small piece of the secret—that the world was older than it should be. This small bit of knowledge had so threatened their power they had set the people howling against us, and helped bring down an empire. As the wise Lord Tharrin was fond of saying, truth is often a brighter lamp than the world cares to see.

I did not like to think what the Good Fathers of the Rhemian Church would do with what the girl could tell them. They greatly covet their hold over the land. If they guessed there was a truth in the world that could put the lie to their teachings, they would move mountains to stop us.

Worse still, there are ever those in power who would suppress a truth, to use it for their own ends. If they guessed the future might be glimpsed. Such creatures as these would care less about a world in chains, than how they might grasp those chains themselves.

There is one thing more, that I have not even shared with my companions. I cannot conceive how Man first sat us on our course, and how he keeps us there. Is there some great clockwork in the earth that guides our fate? Somewhere, there must be. And if it makes us dance like dolls upon a string, *what might it bring to bear against some poor puppet who dares to dance a different tune?*

We cannot say what small and foolish act might pull the world apart. No more, maybe, than the words of a Rhemian girl. I have spent more than one unsleeping night with this.

A sharp whisper broke my thoughts and I rushed to Rhalgorn's side. "There," he pointed, "the boat, Aldair! It is, for certain, though I doubt that you can see it!"

I turned for Signar, but he as already there. "I don't like it. It's the mouth of a river; I can tell by the smell and the wash against our hull."

"Signar, to port!"

"If the depth—" He cut himself off and shook his head,

lumbering off hurriedly to the helmsman. In seconds, we turned, sliding into the easy current. Leaning out, I peered behind us, and could scarcely believe my eyes. Our follower passed us by in the dark, and disappeared to the south.

NINE

Either chance or fortune smiled upon us that night. We neither ran aground nor splintered our hull on some great rock beneath the surface. Instead, we bobbed safe and secure against a relatively light current.

The boat our captive had stolen presented new mysteries. It was afloat, snagged upon vines. There was no sign the female had met with harm, and I doubted she had simply fallen overboard, after safely navigating the open sea. At first light, Signar put parties ashore near the mouth of the river, but she was nowhere to be seen.

"At any rate," Signar pointed out, "why would we find her craft in here, if she beached it near the sea? A boat doesn't float upstream by itself."

And since the shore on either side was choked with greenery to the water's edge, she had evidently made her way upriver and either lost the boat or abandoned it. We would only find out if we followed that path ourselves.

This was no easy task for the *Ahzir,* which had not been built for river work. To make our way we lowered sails and set to poling, the river being too narrow for our oars. As the day came upon us, the air grew stifling hot. The river was brown and murky and smelled of decay. Things roiled unseen beneath the surface, and I assumed—hopefully—these were fishes. Enormous trees grew dark and heavy all around, spreading great canopies over our heads. Only mottled circles of light made their way to the river, painting us all—except the Nicieans—a sickly shade of olive. Vines thick as any

50

creature's arms fell from the heights above, like cables naked from some giant vessel. More than once, we sent crewmen aloft to free us from their grip.

None of us enjoyed the terrible, choking heat of this place, but I supposed the Vikonen suffered the most. Rhalgorn, of course, took the climate as a personal affront to the Stygiann race.

Even in discomfort, we were fascinated by our new surroundings. It was a curious, unfamiliar part of the world. Even the far-sailing Niceans had never ventured here.

"I would guess these lands meet the Great Desert somewhere above us," mused Thareesh. "There are stories which tell of such a place, and it is said that great riches are hidden here."

"Great riches are ever hidden where no one wants to go," Rhalgorn said sourly, wiping sweat from his muzzle. "I have yet to hear of a treasure that puts itself in some convenient place—such as under a fine oak in the woods of the Lauvectii."

I had to laugh at that. "Among the children of the Eubirones, that is exactly where such riches are said to be."

"I am sorry more fat young dinners didn't wander in to find them, then."

I ignored him, listening to the sounds of the green world around us.

Clearly, the strangeness of this place had a most disquieting effect on all aboard. At midday, a fight broke out among the crew. Such a thing is unheard of on the *Ahzir,* and the argument arose from nothing. Once, I spoke to Thareesh about some matter, and he glared at me with fire in his eyes and stalked away. What a repulsive creature, I thought, with his sweet, cloying smell of beetles, and ugly green head. I caught myself, and stopped. Why, I did not feel that way at all about Niceans! What was the matter with me? I shrugged the thought aside, and put it off to our surroundings. We were a somber, brooding crew that day, with little use for ourselves or any other.

By late afternoon we were all too exhausted to care about fighting. Sluggish indifference was the keynote now. I felt like a fool for bringing us on such a useless and dangerous trek. The girl had surely drowned, or been eaten by something, though I did not care to think about that. If she was alive, though, where was she? I was close to telling Signar to get us out of that dismal place and back to sea, when the smothering greenery fell away abruptly and left us under a harsh, open sky again.

We floated upon a brassy lake bordered by tall, straight-boled trees. The shore climbed sharply upward from the water, himming us like the sides of a shallow bowl.

"I don't like the feel of this place," growled Signar. He sniffed the air suspiciously. "It's not right, Aldair. Do you feel it?"

I did, indeed, and every creature aboard sensed it in his bones. This was not what we had experienced on the river—there was far more here than a brooding sense of anger, or irritation. It was a heavy, oppression pall of fear, that lay like a visible thing all about us.

"We'll take a look ashore. A *brief* look," I assured him. "Whatever's wrong with this place, I want little more to do with it."

We did not bring the *Ahzir* to shore. Large gray boulders dotted the shallows, and we rowed our skiff to these and used them as stepping stones. They were close enough together to keep us dry, and handy for leaving the area quickly.

The Stygiann was enjoying himself, hopping from one boulder to the next, then turning about and grinning at us. Thareesh and I tried to ignore this, which was difficult, at best.

We kept a sharp watch ashore, but there was nothing to see except the tall, peculiar trees. The fear, though, was even greater this close to the land. It scratched at every nerve, and set the heart to pounding. Rhalgorn, of course, was not immune to this, but he had decided to show us that Stygianns were not concerned with such things. He continued his bounding until we were nearly to shore, then turned once more to let us see how well he had done. I saw the foolish grin on his face—and saw it suddenly drop away. His jaws fell, and he stared blankly at his feet. The boulder under his boots trembled, shuddered, then rose and sent him howling into the air. A great column of water shot into the air, and rained down upon us.

And there the thing was—no boulder at all but a giant, horrid creature towering over our heads. Thareesh and I fit arrows to our bows. The thing shrieked and bellowed and waved its arms about. It was a great, hulking creature twice the size of a Vikonen, with a broad chest and tree-sized arms and legs. Its skin was gray and cracked like thirsty soil. And if its very size was frightening, that was not the worst of it. Atop its shoulders was a head as big as a barrel, sporting enormous flat ears, tiny black eyes, and a horrible nose that writhed beneath its mouth like a worm. Moreover, on either side of this lengthy snout, a stubby white tooth protruded from its jaws.

For a near eternity, this monster stood there above us, pawing the air, its crushing body blotting out the sun. Then, with a bellow that tore the day away, it turned and splashed ponderously across the shallows and thundered up the hill. It was easy to follow his path, for there was no blade of grass left standing where he passed.

I looked at Thareesh. He stood like a frozen sapling, an arrow taut against his bow, aimed at nothing. "Why didn't you shoot?" I asked. "He was surely an adequate target."

The Niciean relaxed his grip and whipped his thin green tail about his legs. "That is an interesting question," he said. "I was about to ask you the same thing."

I suppose I stared, because he gave me the Niciean version of a foolish grin. Neither of us had an answer. We were both seasoned bowmen, yet we had stood without loosing an arrow. Later, we learned that few men on the decks behind us had found the wits to lift their weapons.

"I am glad I have the protection of such mighty warriors," Rhalgorn said darkly, pulling himself to our boulder. He glared at us both and shook lake water from his pelt. "That was a fine display of courage, friends. What if that whatever-it-was had picked me up and eaten me on the spot? Would either of you killers have lifted a finger?"

Thareesh started to answer, for Niciean soldiers take great pride in their courage. Instead, we all turned our eyes to the hill above. The tall trees that lined the ridge were suddenly alive with terrible creatures. They bellowed and trumpeted and stomped the earth, sending great flocks of colored birds to flight all about the lake. It was an awesome sight to behold, but hardly more bizarre than what followed. In the midst of these monsters, our runaway female suddenly appeared out of nowhere, took one look at our ship below, and came tumbling down to meet us like a long lost relation.

TEN

The Lady's experience with giants had clearly unnerved her, for she ran screaming into my arms, clutched me with a grip of iron, and wailed upon my shoulder. This happy interlude was short lived, of course. She came to her senses immediately and began beating me about the face and cursing me soundly.

"For a moment, you had me worried," I told her. "I thought perhaps those uglies had cast a spell on you. Obviously, this is not true."

"Let *go* of me," she screamed. "Don't you—*dare* put your hands on me, lout!"

Being young and foolish, I continued my efforts to comfort her. This merely drove her to louder outbursts. I was becoming severely bruised about the snout and eyes, and when she began pulling bristles from my jowls I draped her over my shoulder and hauled her back to the ship. For my troubles, I got a quick glimpse of a curly pink tail and other delights, though I was less than interested at the moment.

We would have happily left that place in an instant, but Signar did not wish to try the river in the dark. Instead, we rowed the *Ahzir* to the middle of the lake and anchored there. I gave orders for a fully-armed watch until dawn. As an extra caution, we burned torches on long poles angled over the water. If the monsters tried to approach us, we'd have fair warning, at least.

Our captive went into new fits of hysteria when she learned we were spending the night there. "No, you mustn't!" She

54

shook her head numbly, eyes wide with fear. "You have to get us out of here—now! You—you don't know. They are terrible, terrible creatures!"

"You think they'll come for us, then?" asked Signar.

She gave a nervous little laugh. "You mean attack the *ship?* Of course not. They're scared of you. They're scared of everything!"

"They don't act overly frightened," Rhalgorn said solemnly.

She gave him a haughty toss of her chin and looked away. She was still very fearful of the Stygiann, but she was determined not to show it.

"If any of you oafs would take a moment to *think,*" she sniffed, "you would understand what I'm saying. All that trumpeting and bellowing and thumping about is nothing more than terror. I was with them—I know. They are *scared,* like children. They can't help themselves!"

"They are very large little children," Signar rumbled.

"And heavy," Rhalgorn added. "I would not wish one to fall over me in its fright."

"Just a moment," I said. More wine was poured all around, and I added bread and thick soup to the girl's bowl. She was not too disturbed to eat a double portion of everything. "You say these uglies can't *help* themselves. Just what does that mean?"

"Just what I said. There is an—*aura* of fear about them. A terrible, terrible thing. Haven't you felt it, even out here? I *know* you have. You can't imagine what it's like up close to them."

She told us how she had made her escape, determined to find Rhemian vessels—though she had not really expected help so soon, and had no idea we were being pursued until the first volley of missiles was fired. She pulled into the river, waited awhile, and then decided to strike off inland through the jungle, and make her way back to the beach.

"You could have floated back down," I reminded her. "It was foolish to go wandering about in that place."

She gave me a withering glance. "If I had *floated* back down, you would have seen me. I am *not* stupid, you know."

"No, of course not."

"The monsters captured you, then," Signar prompted.

"Almost the minute I stepped ashore. They have tunnels cleared all through the woods. From the river it looks as if nothing could possibly move in there, but this is not so." She stopped, brought her hands together and looked away. "I can't tell you how awful it is, to be among so many of the things. I wasn't really—captured. I could have left, I think, if there had been any place to go. But I was—scared to try. You're *always* scared when you're with them." She laughed, a little too loudly. "Almost as scared as they are of you!"

"Clearly, she is right," said Thareesh. He had been silent until then. "There is a power in these creatures, Aldair. It was not cowardice that stayed our arrows." He glanced meaningfully at the Stygiann.

"I will be delighted to leave this place," said Signar, "and I doubt we'll have to urge the crew to their posts, either."

A thought occurred to me, and I couldn't help but grin to myself. "Lady," I said, "it appears you could have chosen better jailers the second time around!"

She flushed angrily, turning on me so suddenly I thought she might come across the table for another go at my face. "Could I? Indeed? It may be I was better off with monsters than—than heretics!"

"Ah, you did listen, then."

"Yes, I did." Her chin came up defiantly, and her face fell into a frown. She studied me with a kind of curious loathing. "Are you all truly mad? Do you believe these fantasies, or merely expect others to?"

"They are not fantasies, Lady. I only wish they were."

"Please." She closed her eyes and shook her head. "I am not some farmer's wench who is awed and delighted by nursery tales. I have had some schooling." She gave us all quick glances of amusement. "More, no doubt, than all of you put together."

"No doubt," I said, more than a little weary with this. "And sometimes, Lady, it shows."

She reddened, and gripped her chair. "I would like to go to my quarters now. I've nothing more to say, and there is nothing I wish to hear."

"I fear we'll have to bore you a bit further," I said. "What we are about greatly concerns you now, whether you like it or not. What you heard through that doorway has made you a part of our venture."

She came halfway out of her chair. "You can't know what you're saying! Do you know who I *am?*"

"No. Who are you?"

She sat back down again, breathing hard.

"What you have heard is anything but heresy. It is truth—unpleasant though it may be. And truth is what concerns us here." I looked about the cabin at my companions. "It is well that we have a moment for this. Our guest here departed rather quickly, and cut the story short. There is more, and none of you but Signar has heard it." I stood, moved to the portal and stared out a moment, then turned to face them. "I must tell you now that others share this task of ours. Lord Tharrin was one, his master Nhidaaj the Cygnian another. And one I cannot speak of. I am a link in this chain, as you are. We are searchers, venturers—but others serve in a different manner, such as the scholars we have placed on Albion."

The girl went suddenly pale. "Yes, Lady, this is so. Signar and I traveled through Gaullia and the Northlands, even into Rhemia itself to find learned folk whose minds were not closed to our thinking. There are four of them in those halls below Albion, searching for knowledge that will free us from the bonds of Man."

I looked about, resting finally on the big Vikonen. "To now, only our captain here knows why we sought to pass the Straits into the Southern Sea—and why it is *vital* that we sail to the north again, through every ship the Rhemians bring against us, if need be. There is a lifetime of secrets to be uncovered on Albion. What was its purpose? What did Man build it to do? It is a storehouse of knowledge *about* his manipulation of our history, but what else? Fabius Domitius, who guides our studies there, believes that Albion is only one such stronghold. That there are others. Much of what we might have learned in Albion is lost forever, buried by the years. But one of these places, I am certain, holds the key that will show us *how* Man set us on this dreary path."

"What is the nature of this key," asked Thareesh. "Can we know this?"

"I cannot say," I told him, "for I do not know, for sure. I only know that one such place, like Albion, must lie to the east. Man has left few tracks to follow. But there are some. There is one gray window in Albion, for instance, that pictures him building vast constructions set about with strange devices. There are several of these, but only one is notable for what it tells us. There is sandy wasteland all about, and the sun is fiercely hot."

"The Great Desert, you think?"

"I think it must be, but I cannot say. This is what we must discover."

The girl laughed so harshly she startled us all. "He cannot

say, because there is nothing to *know.* This is all an insanity! By the Creator, you are all as mad as those poor beasts ashore!"

"Beasts we truly are, as I have told you, Lady. But we can be no madder, surely, than the world that Man has left us."

For a moment, I simply stood there, saying nothing. Then, as if the thought had come unbidden, I went to the heavy laquered chest that had once belonged to Lord Tharrin, took the key from about my neck, and opened the fine Niciean lock. I lifted the thing from its velvet case, turned, and held it high against the lamps of the cabin.

It is truly a marvel to see, and there was fear and wonder on their faces. The heavy gold chain is intricately worked, and set about with gems—but it is the pendant itself that catches the eye. It is fashioned in the shape of some beast that never was. It has the scaled body of a Niciean, the wings of a bird, and the head of a creature that reminds me of the being I met in the sands below Xandropolis. Its forelegs are great claws, and its hind legs cloven hooves. It has horns upon its head, and breathes a fire of rubies.

As I held it there, I saw a fire within this beast that was not put there by its maker. It was a fire, I think, that mirrored the great loathing in the eyes of my companions. For this is a thing that was fashioned by Man, and his poisonous touch is still upon it. It is all I have from Albion, save Rhalgorn's sword, and all I want from that place. I took it in defiance of what I saw there.

The Lady did not wish to see this, and turned away. But not, I think, before the spell of it touched her.

ELEVEN

Dawn turned the port above my head a dull and dreary gray. Already, the heat was near to stifling in my cabin, and I wondered what the light of day would bring. One cheery note, at least. The busy sounds on deck said we'd soon be quit of this place, and back to sea. Certainly, not a moment too soon. My head was full of dreams I did not care to remember.

Halfway in my boots, I stopped, and listened again. There was an inordinate amount of noise up there. Something else was afoot, besides the day's work. I jerked a weapon from the floor and hurried topside. Rhalgorn met me at the hatch, his muzzle curved in sly amusement. This is an expression Stygianns like to show whenever possible.

"It appears you have a caller," he said, studying the tips of his fingers. "A very large gentleman, with a nose."

Moving past him, I saw what this was all about. One of the monsters stood just offshore, perched atop a stone. He might have been some troubled artist's notion of a monument to nothing, for he was the same depressing gray as the rock beneath his feet, and the morning itself.

"What do you suppose he wants?"

"A friend, clearly," said Rhalgorn, enjoying this. "He is lonely, and wishes to talk to someone. It may be he is a relative of some sort, Aldair. His snout resembles those of the clan Venicii."

Rhalgorn's humor, as usual, was ill-timed. This was not the day I would have chosen for it. "It may be you are right,"

I said, "for if this is the same fellow we chanced upon yesterday, he has no love for the Lords of the Lauvectii, and handles them with ease."

Signar came up before Rhalgorn could frame an answer. "What do you make of that?"

"A matter we were just discussing."

Signar rubbed his nose. "Well, I'd say, if I was asked, he's wantin' to talk. Though nobody asked me."

Rhalgorn laughed.

"You're right. Nobody did."

"Huh? What'd *I* do?"

"Just get us to shore, if you will—but no closer than you must. There's no use scraping more nerve ends than we have to."

Rhalgorn sobered quickly when he saw I was serious about this. "Aldair, it might be well if I joined you."

"I can surely meet this *relative* without help," I told him shortly. "You had best stay aboard, where you will be dry and safe."

Closer, he was no less frightening than before. A wave of dark, irrational fear washed over me like a fetid wind. There was no true reason for it. It was merely there.

"If you can understand me," I called out to the thing, "just stay where you are and come no closer. If you've something to say, say it." He was at least twenty paces away, and could do me no harm. Still, the moment I spoke, terror clutched my heart. Everything within me cried, *run, run—get back to the ship!* I bit my tongue, and held firm.

"We wants you to be *goes*ing," it cried. "Don't be stayings here no more!"

Its voice had a peculiar, tremulous sound, as if it was carrying small pieces of tin in its mouth. Or, more likely, I supposed, simply talking through its ridiculous nose.

"Don't worry," I assured the creature, "we have no intention of remaining here."

The thing looked alarmed, and its mental message showed it. "No, you doesn't understanding. You got to *goes*, but you mustn't be goes *away!*"

"What's that supposed to mean?"

"Over theres is what wes wanting," it said, pointing across the lake. "You be stayings *real* nice. Over theres. We be seeing your pretty floaterhouse somes."

I stared at him. "You want to—*look* at us?"

"That'll be goods! All right?"

Damn me, I thought, the girl's fair right in what she says. This miserable creature was frightened of everything. Afraid we'd leave. Afraid we wouldn't. Afraid something—Creator knows what—would happen in the next moment or so to scare it further. Children, she had called them, and it was an image that fit too well.

I had not yet answered its question, but from the little jerks of fear it was sending my way, I think it guessed what I would say. I don't know why I persisted in calling *him* an *it*, for he was quite obviously male. Anyone within a Rhemian mile could see that this was so.

I watched him, shifting his big stump legs from one side to the other, and twitching his ugly nose. It was a most repulsive maneuver. He would wind it like a finger about the two protruding teeth, then slide it across his teeth and into his mouth. What, I wondered, was I supposed to say to this creature? Surely, we had little in common. I did not see how we could keep a reasonable conversation going much longer.

Grasping for straws, I noticed he wore something about his neck—an old, battered piece of jewelry, silver and vaguely round, with a small red gem winking at its center. "What is that you're wearing?" I asked politely. "The necklace."

The creature looked up. "This? Is *K'sei*."

"And where did you get it? It's really very nice."

He read the smile, and came close to crying. "Is *K'sei*. Everybody hasing *K'sei!*"

"Oh? Well, fine." So much for that, then. "Does this place have a name? What are your people called? We come from far away and we are not familiar with your land."

"We being Kenyashii," he said simply.

"Kenyashii." They had taken the name of this whole vast continent for themselves, though I doubted they knew this. My next question told me I was right. I asked what lay beyond his lands, and he merely stared at me blankly, as if such a statement had no meaning. No wonder they were terrified—and curious—about outsiders. They had never even seen another race besides themselves!

"We must be leaving very soon now," I told him. The angry wedge of the sun was already peering over the rim of the lake. "We have a long journey ahead of us and—"

The terrible wave of fear nearly brought me to my knees. "You goings? No, is *not* goings!" His big ears shook like the tops of trees, and his huge body trembled. "Can *no* be goings.

You stays! You *stays!*" He raised his enormous head, then, and began to wail. This sorrowful cry echoed across the lake, and back again, where it was taken up by his fellows. I saw them—hundreds—like a thick gray forest spiking the ridge. They swayed to some rhythm only they could hear, trumpeting their painful lament to the world.

Together, their fears were nearly unbearable. I ran across the rocks, my head close to bursting. Signar jerked me aboard, and before my boots touched wood the *Ahzir* was underway, oars churning water for the river. Clearly, we were all of one mind that day.

Even before the green tunnel closed around us, crewmen who had no other duties rushed to help the polers with their work. Soon, there were no more poles to go around, and they grabbed our long oars to use, jamming them deep into the muddy bottom. Signar's roar put a stop to this, but not before several oars were snapped in two, or lost.

I did not blame our people for their actions. A fear they couldn't fathom swarmed about their heads like angry bees. Only the Creator himself could have moved us from that place fast enough to suit us.

Still, I told myself, we are away. And every moment takes us further. This fear will fade, and we will leave it far behind . . .

Only—it wasn't *happening* that way at all. I realized, suddenly, that if anything it was greater than before! How could that be? Did the Kenyashii's thoughts linger like dust upon the stifling air, even after they were gone? I knew this wasn't so, for we had not been greatly bothered the night before, in the middle of the lake.

"I feel it," said Thareesh, guessing my thoughts. His words rustled in my ear like dry paper. "It is with us, still." He stood perfectly still, as a Niciean will do sometimes. A small vein pumped at the base of his throat. "Something is wrong," he hissed finally, "very wrong indeed, Aldair!"

Past him, I saw a Vikonen seaman stop in his tracks and go rigid. Black agate eyes looked at nothing, and a deep rumble shook his chest.

I heard it, then. Nothing. No sound at all. The jungle had gone abruptly silent. I took a breath, held it.

Suddenly, Thareesh moved like lightning. I jerked around, saw Rhalgorn frozen above me, gray hackles standing straight upon his back, lips bared in a snarl. Faster than I could follow, one of the long lances which are set about the decks was in his hands and gone. A high squeal of pain came back from the jungle. Rhalgorn's battle cry tore the air.

Then, the whole world exploded around us.

Wood split with a crack like thunder and a great tree came crashing into the river. Water sprayed the deck like rain, and our prow hit hard, slamming us to ground and sucking the breath from our lungs. Timber groaned and shrieked. I heard good Signar roar, his cry lost beneath the wild trumpeting of the Kenyashii. Arrows and lances hummed through the still air, but few found their mark. The monsters were well hidden under a thick curtain of green.

Something enormous shattered itself to death in the jungle. I looked up, watched the bole of some immense tree roll toward us in a lazy, sluggish arc, then crash upon the decking aft. Damn, I thought, we're split in half for sure!

They had chosen their spot with care. The river narrowed and there was scarcely room on either side of our hull. Signar bellowed orders. Big Vikonen crewmen sprang from our decks to hack us free. Their great axes sang while archers watched above them, sending a deadly swarm into the green. And, as suddenly as it began, it was over.

Other creatures would have trapped us there and killed us off from the jungle. But the Kenyashii were not fighters— fear, and not a lust for blood, ruled their lives. They had little heart for battle, and when our weapons began to hum about their heads they fled through their shadowy tunnels, until we could hear their cries no more.

When at last we were well downriver and away, Signar reported that we had been more than lucky to come out of the fray in one piece. "The bow's some cracked, but we had no great speed when we hit. I can mend it while we're underway, and it'll hold if we have fair weather." He looked up, hoping some North-god had heard him.

The afterdeck was in ruin, but it would not affect our passage. We had been fortunate, indeed, that one of the Kenyashii's trees had not snapped our masts away. That would have put us in a pretty fix for sure, for it is no easy matter to find the proper wood for a good mast—and it is even harder to set these great columns into place.

One crewman's leg was broken. Another had cracked his head but would recover. We had a wealth of leaves and branches scattered about, and when we sailed out of the river and into the sea, we were still tossing debris over the side.

It was during this activity that Signar bellowed out my name and brought me running forward. He said nothing, but merely growled and pointed with great disgust. Amid a spray of vines and branches, the Kenyashii was spread out upon the deck like an enormous pile of dirty sacking, a bump the size of a small boulder swelling the back of his head.

TWELVE

There is seldom peace for the venturer. He who goes beyond his well for water, say the oldsters of the Eubirones, can look to find a bitter drink. In truth, this may be so.

Once clear of the river we should have been quit of the Kenyashii. Instead, we now played host to one of these ugly creatures on our decks. We should have been glad to face the sea again—instead, we searched the bright horizon with concern, knowing we had not been forgotten by our Rhemian friends.

"We could sight their sails at any moment," Signar said gloomily, "and this would not surprise me. The Rhemians are ignorant in many ways, but they are not entirely witless creatures. They will know by now we are not to the south, that we have turned to the Straits again. They will hound us to death, Aldair. What the Niciean has said is true. The sea is theirs, now."

I looked past him, seeking answers on a crest of foam. For a moment I fancied we were well beyond the Rhemian vessels—that Signar was wrong, and the sea was free of enemies.

"What would you have me do?" I asked him. "Our way is clear. We *must* pass the Straits to the east!"

"Aldair—" Thareesh laid slim fingers on my arm and urged me to his side. Taking his dagger, he scratched lightly on the cover of a hatch, then looked up again. "We have fought beside each other in the Great Desert. There is much good blood between us, and I will openly admit you are near as good an archer as I." A slight grin creased the slit of his mouth. "I know the import of this mission. But, like Signar, I see much ill fortune ahead, if we continue on our path."

"If?" I stood back from him. "There can be no *if* in this, good friend."

"A moment. I would say what I have in mind. Here—" He gestured at his scratchings. "This is the Southern Sea, Niciea and the boot of Rhemia. Here is the land of Kenyarsha. One way to the east lies through the Straits. Another, perhaps—" He swept the tip of his blade in an arc around the blob he called Kenyarsha, back to the eastern shore of the Southern Sea.

I stared. "Go *around*, Thareesh? There are no *maps* of Kenyarsha. We don't even know what it looks like. It might take weeks, months. Even then, our route might take us no-where *near* the east!"

"Kenyarsha might be smaller than we think," Signar mumbled hopefully.

"Or larger!" I snapped irritably. "No. We *cannot* take such a chance. If we were merely sailing for our pleasure, fine. But there is too much at stake here."

"A wise decision," the Vikonen said sourly. "We trade unknown seas and possible failure for near certain disaster."

"You don't know this is so!"

They looked at me, but said nothing. Good and true companions—but for the moment, I could not face them, and didn't care to. Surely, I told myself, when a person turns from friends in anger, it is time to turn to himself, and take a closer look. "You must understand that I—cannot put this task aside. My feelings on this color my words. And my manners as well."

Signar made a noise. "Manners be damned, Aldair. Good sense is what counts, and little else. We could be wrong in this—but so could you. Whatever we do, we'd best be right the first time."

"Signar— Wait for me, the both of you. There's something I must do, and there's no better time for it than now."

She opened the portal with her usual cool disdain. It was the only weapon she had against us, but she used it well. "Lady, I will get right to the point, since I know you are less than interested in conversation. I would know who you are. Now. Without argument or lies. I have no time to play games, or plead with you."

She threw back her head and laughed. "What's the matter,

heretic? You are not beginning to worry about Rhemian justice, are you? It would be well if you did, for you shall surely taste it soon!"

She was a pretty thing, but probably the most aggravating female on earth. Why do we place such great value on creatures whose only aim is to reduce us to witless fools? In truth, I suppose we get what we deserve. We have placed them at such low station in life, they have great incentive to drag us down with them. And usually, we are all too willing to make the trip.

"I see I was right in the first place," I told her. "You will never listen to reason."

"I will never listen to *anything* you might have to say!"

"Fair enough, then." Turning from her, I opened the port nearby to show her Rhalgorn standing outside. He grinned at her, showing his teeth. The Lady went suddenly pale.

"You—wouldn't!"

"I admit, it is a terrible thing to do to a friend, but it is a guilt I will have to bear. In time, he will no doubt forgive me. Now," I said, moving for the door, "I will leave you two together. Simply call me when you have an answer."

Suddenly, she was quite full of answers. She spoke so rapidly, about so many things, I could scarce remember the half of what she said.

For a moment, I stood upon the deck breathing lungfuls of clean salt air. As Rhalgorn might say, it would not be seemly to appear ill in front of the crew.

"Aldair, is something the matter?" asked Signar.

"Nothing that can be helped," I told him. "You will be pleased to know that you were right about the Rhemians. They will most certainly hound us to the ends of the earth. You had best steer south, and pray there is a way around Kenyarsha, for it seems that I have stolen Corysia, niece of the Emperor Titus Augustus. Why, Signar, do I have such an unerring talent for disaster?"

THIRTEEN

The Kenyashii are not only the largest creatures in the world, but the smelliest, as well. It is difficult to surpass a crew of burly Vikonen, together in a stuffy tavern after months at sea. Or a Stygiann warrior, in full battle odor. But these are offenses of a different nature, and can be tolerated in time.

A Kenyashii is something else again. His smell is born of fear, and there is nothing which more foully poisons the body. This would not be particularly troublesome in a frightened mouse. But given a creature the size of a Kenyashii, and you have something to contend with, even on the open decks of a ship at sea.

It is never easy to talk to these creatures—their minds seem to work in a wholly different manner. This, plus their overpowering odor, and constant emanations of fear, makes conversation next to impossible.

"You must stop what you are doing," I told the thing, standing as far back as I could, and still make myself heard. "You are disrupting the ship, and I will not have it!"

"Is not likings it here," he moaned. "Wants to be no *stayings!*"

"You will simply have to put up with it for the moment. If we did not have to make time, I assure you we'd have you out of here in a minute."

"Wants to do thats *now!*" It began to make that bizarre, nerve-grinding noise again, bellowing through its nose. Fear swept over me on the crest of nauseous odor. Holding my head, I staggered back a pace.

"Stop that! Damn you, you have no *reason* to be afraid. Don't you understand *any*thing?" Evidently it did, for the pounding in my head eased slightly.

"Juumb'ar can goes home?" he asked hopefully.

"Is that your name? Juumb'ar?"

"If you likings all right. Can be some elses if you wants."

"If I *like* it? Why on earth should I care what you call yourself?"

The Kenyashii pulled in his shoulders and studied me with tiny black eyes, then stuck his nose in the corner of his mouth. "You likes me some betters, now, than befores?"

"Befores—before what?"

"When we was talkings."

"When do you mean? I don't—" Then, it struck me what he meant. "That was you? On the rock, in the lake? No, I'm afraid I like you a great deal less, if anything. That was a treacherous thing to do, Juumb'ar—we meant no harm to your people, and you had no provocation to attack us."

"Kenyashii wasn't attacks no one," he wailed, "just *helping* you from *goesing*. You should be stays. Should not be *goes!*" With that, he started waving his arms and legs around in wild, erratic arcs, shrieking through his nose.

"Damn you," I shouted, "stop that—at once!" In answer, this immense heap of flesh began to tremble and shudder uncontrollably, writhing about on the decks. A hot stream of liquid struck me full in the chest, near spilling me off my feet. I stood there, stunned, a dreadful, pungent odor making its way to my nostrils. Finally, I began to understand what this great lout had done to me, though I could scarcely believe that such a thing could happen.

It was vital that we put leagues behind us, now that we were committed to our course. Neither Signar nor I felt the Rhemians would pursue us south, through uncharted waters. We could not be sure, of course, now that we knew the name of our royal guest. The Rhemians are a stubborn people. At any rate, we had the open sea ahead, and fair winds behind. For the first time, I felt our mission was truly underway. We would not be thwarted in this task. If there was a way around Kenyarsha, we would find it.

There was, of course, still one barrier to our progress. What I'd told Juumb'ar was true—we would have put him ashore in an instant if we could have done so with safety. Unfortunately, the shallows to port looked less than inviting, and with our prow still weakened, we were less than anxious to damage it further.

After our third day at sea, however, Signar was ready to sail the *Ahzir* over mountains, if necessary. "Let's get him off of here, Aldair. One way or the other. We've a good crew aboard, but you can't ask 'em to fight the sea, and that thing, all at once. I've got two or three fights a day on my hands, and more in the making. There'd be worse than that, I fear, if half the lads weren't down with fevers of one sort or another."

"You can blame the fights on our oversized friend," I told him, "but the fever's from the river. We've all had a touch of that."

Signar growled and shook his big shoulders. "It's not the fevers and the fights so much. It's the—other things."

"What other things?"

"Well, the dreaming and all."

"I know about that. It's the Kenyashii. What else, Signar?"

He frowned and scratched his pelt. "Some of the crew are —seeing things."

"Seeing things? What kind of things?"

The Vikonen hesitated. "Strange things. Awful looking creatures walking about on deck at night. Things with—eyes and arms all over. Comin' out of the sea."

I stared at him, saying nothing.

"Aldair, I've seen 'em myself," he said darkly. "I wouldn't admit this to another living person, but I'll tell you true. I saw this thing, just before the sun. It sat upon the prow and mocked me, calling out in some strange tongue." He ran a hand across his muzzle. "I don't pretend to understand such things. I only know what I saw with my own two eyes. Whatever terrible gods that monster's set upon us, they're stronger than our own."

I shook my head. "What you saw was less than real, Signar. If Juumb'ar can project his fears upon us, I suppose he can conjure up false visions of these frights as well. They do not come from his gods—only from his own poor frightened mind."

"So?" The Vikonen gave me a frown. "What difference does it make, where they come from? Another night of this

and we'll have a witless crew on our hands—and likely a
captain, too, though it shames me to say it!"

"Does the shore still look as bad for landing?"

"Worse."

Clearly, this was a thing that had to be. "Keep the watch
alive. If we don't find a spot by morning, we'll have to put
him over."

"Aldair. There is nothing else for it."

"No, there is not. And if it must be done, I will do it."

I myself had suffered dreams and fretful sleep, but had
seen no spectral visions. If Rhalgorn noted ghostly creatures
bumping about, Stygiann pride would not allow him to say
so. Thareesh admitted that he *might* have seen something—
but wouldn't say what. The Lady Corysia, of course, had
nothing to say to me on this subject or any other.

We drank dark ale that night, and dined on lentil soup
and good potato bread. Thareesh had stocked our larders
well, and there was even fresh meat aboard—the flesh of
some deer-like animal that thrives in the rocky wastes about
the Southern Sea. I am no great meat eater, but Signar and
the Stygiann relished this treat. A full belly put Rhalgorn in
rare humor—he told outrageous lies, and did an imitation
of a Niciean catching bugs with his tongue that even brought
a laugh from the usually somber Thareesh. It may be that we
all laughed a great deal more than either ale or entertainment
called for. There was a pall upon the night, like the breathless quiet that presses the sea to murky glass before the storm.

When the Kenyashii began to shriek and howl above, we
left our table quickly, without words, as if this outcry was a
thing expected—the first far touch of lightning that would
break our spell.

The creature was trembling and thrashing about on the
deck. Dark liquid spilled from its mouth and nose. A terrible
stench was in the air, and this time it was something more
than fear. The thing had fouled itself, then writhed about in
its own filth.

Rhalgorn muttered something under his breath. Signar
framed an answer, but words never came. A crewman
shouted, thrusting a shaky finger off the stern.

We all saw it, and there was no mistaking what it was. A
dark, spectral ship ran silently in our wake, no more than a
length behind. It was long and slender, with a dolphin prow
and crescent sails. There were creatures on its deck—somber,

terrible things that seemed to have no bones about them.
Each was dressed in cold and icy armor; quicksilver weapons
glittered at their sides. Empty eyes stared out from frozen
helms, glowing with a pale and deathly light that touched
the ship itself, and brushed its ashen sails. We did not need
the name upon her bow to tell us who she was, for this was
clearly the *Ahzir al'Rhaz.* And if that vessel was the ghost of
our own, its crew were the shades of ourselves.

Beside me, an old Rhemian sailor went white as snow.
Fright and anger curled his jaw, and a blade slid to his hand.
"Kill him," he cried, *"kill the damned thing!"* Others took
up his call and surged as one toward the Kenyashii. I tried
to shout, but no words came. I could feel things happening
around me, but I could do nothing to stop them. I felt as if
I were living a breath or two ahead of the world; that what
occurred here was already a heartbeat behind. Thus, I saw
the crew move forward, weapons in their hands, and saw the
thing spring up out of nothing in their midst. It curled like
autumn smoke from dry and brittle leaves, and where it
touched, hearts went cold. Through its milky form I heard a
big Vikonen's thunder-cry; another crewman clawed his way
unthinking to the rail and leaped into the sea. One good
friend fell upon another, and tore bare flesh to tatters.

Fear stalked our decks and we were helpless before it. The
dread thing snaked its way among us, and each saw his own
worst terrors come to life. Awesome towers, with blind and
empty windows . . . beasts that never were . . . loathsome
things that rolled up from the sea to pull us to its depths.

Signar lifted his great axe against the Kenyashii—something only he could see set him roaring, then tossed him to
the decks like a child. Juumb'ar wailed in pain and thrashed
about. I looked, and saw the thing about his throat flash dully in the ghostly light. The blood-red jewel that sat upon it
seemed to wink like a tiny eye. I stared into it for the small-
est part of a moment, and saw a thing I did not want to see.

I moved unthinking, shuting my mind to all about me. I
thought of lazy afternoons by the River Brundus, when big
fat fish leaped upon the shore to be caught . . . crisp winter
days when frost tipped the morning. And when I reached
the Kenyashii I clawed out blindly and tore that thing from
its neck. It burned, like cold fire. I yearned to toss it from
me, but could not. There were things to see there—terrible,
beautiful things, dreams no creature ever dreamed before.

A thousand lifetimes later, Rhalgorn ripped it from my

grip and flung it to the sea. His war-howl followed it through the darkness until it fell out of sight beneath the waters.

And then—nothing. Even the shadow of fear was gone. There were neither ghosts aboard nor spectral ships behind. Only the starry night and the sea.

FOURTEEN

The day dawned bright and clear, but it would be more than a while before the sun washed all the shadow from our hearts. The night had left us poorer. One crewman had fled to the safety of the deep. Two were gravely injured and would surely die. Another was simply frozen in fear, and would likely never get his wits about him.

Juumb'ar lay upon the deck, still as death, for two full days. We knew, now, that he was not to blame for his fears, and the havoc they had caused among us. But when good companions die, it is easy to fix the blame where you can clearly see it. It is to the credit of the crew—and Signar's presence—that this creature did not gain a fresh new mouth beneath his own.

Certainly, we cursed ourselves for not guessing the cause of our sorrow earlier. Who could have known that Juumb'ar's amulet was at fault? It is always easier to see the way a puzzle's put together when it's finished. Now, we could imagine what had likely happened here: the creature's horror at being away from his own, and at sea, had so intensified his fears they had nearly overwhelmed us all.

Juumb'ar himself could add nothing to this, for when he awoke, he remembered nothing. It was a full week before he would speak at all—and then, for some time, only to Thareesh. In the eye of the Kenyashii, the Niciean's calm and easy manner outweighed his bizarre appearance.

"All he knows is that his people have always worn the thing. Each is given an amulet at birth, and wears it through-

74

out his life. As one might guess, they believe this gift to come from the gods."

"It would be better, I think, to have no gods at all," said Rhalgorn.

"This is so," Thareesh agreed, "but only the very wise or very foolish chose their own higher powers. These poor creatures not only place their lives in bondage to this thing, they go to great lengths to assure that none of their people are without it." He explained, to our horror, that the total population always equaled the number of amulets available.

"If an amulet ceases to function—which has happened several times within memory—a member of the tribe is eliminated. There are no more than a hundred or so of Juumb'ar's people left, though I suspect there is another reason for this, besides the scarcity of amulets. They have been breeding in ever smaller numbers over the years, and no longer produce many young." He looked at us a moment, flicking his tongue in the Nicíean manner. "They cannot last as a people much longer, unless they cease to enslave themselves. And this is not likely. The poor fellow on our deck wants only one thing from us now—the chance to place that damnable thing *back* about his throat. Can you believe this? He has lived an illusion so long he cannot face the world without his fears!"

Signar shook his great head. "For the life of me, I can't see how a folk'd get themselves into such a mess, 'less some fool *made* 'em do it in the first place."

"Like the iron collar of slavery," said Thareesh.

"Only worse."

"I think Signar has come close to the truth," I said. "I believe the Kenyashii indeed gained this bondage from another. One we about this table know too well."

For a moment, they showed me only puzzled faces. Then, understanding found them all. "I would have spoken of this before, but I wished to hear the creature's words, if we could. As I told you, when I looked into the small red eye it held me there, and I could not look away from it. It promised me great and terrible fears. Still, I did not wish to let it go. I wanted these things. I *wanted* to be afraid! Now, I am near as certain as I can be. Where else could such a horror come from? And who but Man could make it?"

Thareesh shook his head. "That is too long in the past, Aldair. It could not be. Nothing—"

"Nothing?" I cut him off, kicking back my chair and moving to a port. I breathed in fresh sea air. "Nothing indeed, in the world we know, could wink like a bloody eye and loose a flood of fear on all who look upon it. —Unless it came from Man. Albion is a hundred centuries old, or older —and it is full of such wonders, near as perfect now as ever. And there is one thing more that's lasted: you, me, and every creature on the earth, living out our lives in the pattern of Man. We are all the proof that's needed. And no, I don't believe the Kenyashii have worn the amulets since they were changed from beasts and set here. Thareesh was right in that. The *amulets* could last—but not the Kenyashii. How they found them, and where, we'll likely never know. It's a secret bound up in the past."

Signar's fist shook the table. "Who*ever* wore 'em first, the Kenyashii or some other, I can damn well guess what they were for, and so can you all. Why, they're just the thing for keeping some poor beast in line, when you don't want him running all about. Even better 'n pens and fences!"

It was not a pretty image. I am sure my companions saw themselves in such a setting, as I did.

Our ill-fated journey upriver was two full weeks in the wake of the *Ahzir*. Every day we expected the land of Kenyarsha to bend, and point us north again. Clearly, it was a greater continent than we'd imagined; the green line to port gave every indication of going on forever.

"I hope I have not led us into nothing," Signar said gloomily. "If I am right, we've already traveled more leagues than lie between Vikonea and the Straits."

"All that proves is that it is some further than that to where we are going," I told him. Whether such remarks gave Signar added confidence, I cannot say. They did precious little for me.

Our supplies were not dangerously low, but there was nothing overly fresh left in our larder. This is one aspect of sea travel that is displeasing to me. It does not take long to eat up everything that tastes good.

One morning, we found a sparkling blue inlet where we could clearly see ripe fruits bending the trees. Unfortunately, something very big and loud had found this haven too, and didn't welcome our intrusion. We never saw it plainly, but we could watch it stomp about behind the trees, guarding its keep. A day later, we found another site, with no large resident on hand. The fruit was not as plentiful, but we picked what we could find, and filled our kegs with fresh water.

Something strange occurred while we were anchored in that place, and I set it down here as it happened, without great understanding. The night was cool and full of stars, and I stood upon the deck and breathed the sweet air from off the land. I had spent some time below, bringing the chronicle of our ventures up to date as best I could, for I had been most remiss in this. The hour was late, and there was no other soul about except the watch. I was surprised, then, when I sensed someone behind me, and turned—to face myself.

I was startled, to say the least. But strangely, only for a moment, and without fear. It was a dim, hazy apparition, ringed with an aura of blue. It stood there before me, this other Aldair, then set its hands upon the railing and gazed to shore. The clothes it wore were strange to me—certainly, nothing of my own. It neither spoke nor made any other kind of sound, but kept its eyes upon the shore as if it searched for something there. Finally, it turned to face me, and I thought for sure that it would speak. Instead, it simply vanished, as if it had never been.

Toward the morning, I slept, and dreamed deeply. And when I awoke I set the crew to bringing that dream to life, as I had seen it. I took the pendant of the beast of Albion, sketched it as true as I could, and gave this to them, instructing them to paint the image on our mainsail, and on the face of their shields. I cannot say why I did this, only that it greatly pleased me when it was done. The crew viewed this emblem with great pride, and readily accepted it as the ensign of the *Ahzir*.

I cannot properly explain either of these happenings. Why the other Aldair came to me, or what impelled me to set that image before the world. Perhaps the first never happened. Or perhaps the setting of that sign is what he was about. In truth, I cannot say.

During this time, I spoke only once to Juumb'ar, and this out of necessity. Admittedly, he was somewhat more pleasant than before, but this is saying little. Perhaps, in time, when his fears fell away and he had the chance to see the world as it was, he would change. We could only wait and see. Rhalgorn stated flatly that there was no need in waiting—the Kenyashii were basically repulsive and would always remain so. This, from an expert on the subject.

Both Signar and the Stygiann urged me to put him ashore, but I would not do this against his will. He was harmless now, and a completely helpless creature. Once, I had been ready to put him over the side when he was a danger to us all. Now, though, I did not have the heart to send him to a certain death in the wilds of Kenyarsha.

"Wants to be goesing home now, Aldair," he told me. "Is better wes turning floaterhouse backs up other way."

"Juumb'ar, we would all like to go home. Someday, we will."

"But not *nows?*"

"No, not now."

"Wheresit we be goings, Aldair?"

"That way."

"Juumb'ar doesn't *wants* to go that way. Wants to goes *home!*"

"Thareesh talked to you about that, remember? He said you could go ashore if you liked. You do not have to stay here."

Tears welled up in his tiny eyes. "Thareesh is means and ugly foy saying thats, too. Juumba'r can't bes walking backs home in scarey places. Doesn't *likes* that!"

"Then I suggest you resign yourself to some sailing."

"Sailings make me *sick*, Aldair. This bes a *bad* floaterhouse!"

"Nevertheless, it is *our* floaterhouse, and we all live together on it. Which leads me to a subject we must discuss. Thareesh has spoken to you several times about this, but you evidently refuse to listen. Since we *are* all here together, you must cease defecating on the decks. This is not our custom aboard sailing vessels, and it should be quite obvious why. Moreover, you are a rather large creature. When you do not follow these rules, the problem is doubly—or triply—compounded."

"Doesn't likes to get near the edges of the floaterhouse, Aldair. Is a scarey being place!"

"Still, you *will* get near the edge, Juumb'ar. Or over it."

So I left him, wailing and trumpeting his sorrows. Perhaps this brief example shows just why I did not encourage conversation between us.

FIFTEEN

One day before we had been at sea a full three weeks, our lookouts brought us all to port with the cry of open sea ahead. It was an awesome thing to behold. Great winds howled about this cape, thrusting mighty combers ashore. The sea churned around us like a kettle put to boil, and it was easy to believe we had truly reached the end of the world. What lay south, I wondered—the edge of the earth, where the sea falls off into nothing? Or did the world go on forever, to one far land after another?

For the most part, we had long since left familiar stars behind. Both the Axe and the Limping Slave, which shine overhead in the cold skies of the Northland, had near disappeared in our wake. Only the head of the Slave peeked over the night horizon. Now, there were new mysteries in the sky, brilliant clusters of ice and fire which had no names for us. If we had not possessed the magic needle, which is known to Niceans, and not others, we might have been lost in these waters. It was a comfort to see it point unerringly north, even at the end of the world.

Dolphins and great whales sported in these waters, and this was one of the few diversions that brought a smile to the Lady Corysia. We had seen much more of her lately—a long sea voyage can be rather boring if you stay to yourself. Thus, she even graced our table on occasion, though she contributed little there but an appetite.

"They are so delightful," she laughed, "so alive and free!"

I watched her, the sea breeze whipping about her garments

and pressing her soft ears against her head. She had the fetching habit of wrinkling her snout when she laughed, and each time this occurred, something stirred within me. We are what we are, I suppose. I could no more help but want her, than she could help loathing the ground I walked on.

"Freedom is a thing all creatures long for," I said, coming up beside her. "It is a gift more precious than life itself."

She turned, one brow feigning surprise to find me there. "I suppose that was meant to be an affront to me, Master Aldair?"

"In no way, Lady. You must try not to be overly sensitive about being Rhemian. You were born that way, and can't help it. Any more than I can help being a kidnapper, traitor, heretic, pirate, barbarian—what else was there?"

She flushed, then sighed resignedly and turned back to her whales.

"Lady, I'm sorry," I told her. "We are ever at each other, like two small children."

She faced me with a thoughtful, near melancholy smile. "In truth, what else could we be? We are worlds apart, you and I. If it is any comfort," she added mischievously, "I no longer blame *you* for being—all those things. The other, by the way, was villain."

"Ah, of course. Thank you."

"You are welcome."

We both laughed, but this rare moment ended abruptly. She realized, with some alarm, that she had let her better nature get the best of her.

"Look," I said quickly, "that business about freedom had little to do with Rhemia. I was referring to our quest, this voyage."

"I am not interested in this voyage, except to see the end of it."

"And our quest, of course, is a lie."

"Most certainly."

"That's quite interesting."

"And why do you think so?"

"I have had some education myself, Lady. Nothing so fine as the Seven Schools of Rhemia, but there were good Masters at Silium. At least, they taught us that our heads were supposed to do more than decorate our shoulders."

"You are trying to tell me something," she said coolly, "though I doubt you'll get to the point of it."

"The point, Lady, is that while you do not have to credit

my tale of Island Albion, you can scarce ignore what happened *here*, on this ship. *How* did this happen—through magic? My good Master Levitinus, rest his soul, would say 'Aldair, the educated person looks first to reason, for even the mysteries of this world that *seem* to smack of black powers, merely follow unseen laws of their own.' Did this thing of the amulet happen, Lady, or did it not? Reason tells us it did."

Corysia faced me. "There are things we do not understand in this world. I grant you that. But a man finds ways to wrap the mantle of reason about his follies, to lend them respectability."

"You would know about respectability, Lady. It is a word that covers a multitude of Rhemian sins."

Her hand came swiftly from the railing. It stung me once, and would have again. I grabbed her hands and clamped them to her sides.

"You are truly a man," she laughed haughtily. "How marvelous that you can hold one small woman by yourself!"

"Lady, that is the second time this day you have called me 'man.' It is not a word I care for. If you had the sense the Creator gave a turnip, you'd know the reason why!"

With that, she tore away and fled to her cabin. Thus ended another of our conversations, in the usual manner.

The third day after rounding Kenyarsha, we ploughed northward through increasingly heavy seas. Our bow rose high, scattering brine like a tattered veil, then plunged back to sea with a shudder that near jarred us to the bone. Signar said it was only the tail of a storm that had moved inland the day before. I was glad we had not seen the rest of it.

When the winds let go at last, we were far from our course, and out to sea. The land was to the west of us, now, and we set our sails for the sight of it. However, we had not counted on the perversity of weather at sea. The wind fell completely away. Not a breath stirred anywhere, and our sails hung limp as laundry. Thus, we took to oars again, making way for land, and waiting for a breeze.

It was hard going, with no air to cool our labors. The crew moaned and grumbled and swore the sea had turned to syrup. After an hour of this, Signar called a halt, and hailed me to the foredeck. "If you think this is hard going," he growled, "you are right. Here, look at this." He tossed a chip of wood into the sea. Then another. Our oars were raised and there was no air stirring. Yet, the chips moved past us swiftly to the north and east.

"There is nothing moving above the water," Signar explained, "but there is a great deal going on below. We are in some sort of current, and a swift one."

"What do you suggest?"

"I do not suggest anything," he said sourly. "I am a captain, but I have nothing to captain at the moment. We can row our hearts out, but we will go nowhere. We will have to wait. There is nothing else for it."

"What's the longest you have ever been becalmed?" I asked.

"Oh, fourteen or fifteen days. But that is quite unusual."

"I'm glad to hear it."

"Of course, I know nothing of these waters. It may be quite common here."

"I am sure it isn't," I told him. "I know nothing of these waters either, but it does not appear to be that kind of place to me."

Later, I was not entirely certain of this. For four days, not a breath of air stirred the water. From dawn until well after sunset we roasted like bugs on a stone, moving only when we had to. The nights were not much better. We were on short water rations, which didn't help. Some of our crewmen found comfort in swimming around the ship, but this pleasure was short-lived when our lookouts reported more great sharks than they could count circling just beyond the swimmers.

The Nicieans could stand the sun better than most of us, but they did not like to show themselves in the heat of the day. Their favorite time was just before the dawn, when they would make a game of chasing one another through the rigging, scampering up and down the masts as fast as the eye could follow, leaping from one dizzy perch to another. It was a marvel to see, for there are no better climbers in the world.

On the fifth day, low clouds appeared to the south. As they approached, a damp, hot wind stirred our sails, but it was hardly enough to matter. Finally, the clouds simply vanished in a copper sky.

"I would think a seaman, who is used to this sort of business, would *do* something," Rhalgorn complained. "It is not seemly to merely sit here."

Signar gave him a broad grin. "Well, now, what would you

suggest? what does one do when he is becalmed in the forest of the Lauvectii?"

Rhalgorn showed his teeth. "We are not foolish enough to play with boats in the Lauvectii. Thus, nothing like this ever happens."

"Ships," Signar corrected.

"What?"

"We are on a *ship*, as I have told you before—not a *boat*."

"Whatever we are on," Rhalgorn sniffed, "it is not going anywhere. Even a land person can see that."

At dawn, on our seventh day without wind, the watch brought us all to the deck with a shout. Each newcomer added his dry-throated cheer to the rest as we watched banks of heavy white clouds pile up in the south.

"Surely there is a wind or two in that," said Thareesh.

Signar roared, picking up the startled Niciean in his great arms and shaking him like a stick. "There is, indeed, friend—enough to sail us clear to the end of the world!"

"We have already done that," Rhalgorn reminded him. "It would be sufficient if you could sail us back to the other end. We are—" He stopped, his gaze narrowing to the sky. "Look there," he pointed, "south, but east as well."

Shading my eyes, I followed his gaze. There were dots, dark against the clouds. "I see nothing, save a flock of birds."

Rhalgorn made a noise. "To you, perhaps. To Stygiann eyes, they are more than merely birds. They fly, but they are near as big as I am, Aldair."

"He is right," said Thareesh.

"Of course I am right. There is nothing new in that."

Soon, even those with lesser vision could see that this was so. Signar muttered something to his mate and our archers took their posts. Other crewmen lifted lances at the ready.

Nearly twenty of the creatures circled high above us now in twos and threes. There was no doubting they were more than birds. There was an order about their flight, and purpose in their actions. They were greatly interested in who we were and what we were doing, but they took their time approaching.

"Rhalgorn—are they armed? Do they carry any weapons you can see?"

"They have nothing about them that would harm us," he said. "Some carry little packets about their necks, but nothing more."

With that, I gave the order to lay our arms aside. We could take them up again, if need be. The flying creatures understood this immediately. They clustered all together, like a swarm of bees, then one circled down upon us in a long, easy glide. Twice, he crossed our bow to look us over, flying no higher than our mainmast. Then, quite suddenly, he turned and dropped swiftly to the deck. For a moment, we thought he'd fall like a stone and flatten himself—then, powerful wings took hold and drummed the air, slowing him to an easy, graceful landing. Startled, I realized I had seen these creatures once before. Just a glimpse, in the gray windows below Albion. Here, then, was another mockery of Man.

Our visitor was a strange being indeed, but I am sure that we seemed stranger still—heavy, clumsy and earthbound, while he soared the skies at will. He was tall, but outlandishly gaunt; arms and legs so delicately thin I was sure he'd break like a stick to the touch. His only strength lay in his broad, powerful wings. He was as lost upon the ground as I was in the air.

He waited, perfectly still. I walked out to meet him slowly, so he would not be alarmed. He watched me with sad golden eyes. A crest of crimson feathers topped his skull, then faded to pink over a sharp, horny beak. This crest was the only color about him. The rest of his body was covered uniformly in gray feathery down.

"My name is Aldair," I told him. "You may rest easy, friend. No one aboard will harm you."

The golden eyes blinked once. "I am Rhaiz, and I did not think that you would harm me. It is said you come in peace."

"*Said?*" I stared at him. "Someone—told you we were coming?"

Rhaiz shook his head. "It is not necessary to be told such a thing. It has been written that you would come." He spread his feeble arms. "Now, you are here."

SIXTEEN

Rhaiz explained that his people were from a land to the north and east called Indrae, only a short flight away. Signar, who has a head for these things from many years at sea, judged we could sail under a good wind at three-quarters the speed of our flying friends.

"It's less than a day away," he said, "if my figures are right. It'd be a fair good idea, Aldair, to put into this place."

This, of course, was his own peculiar way of expressing our dire need for rest, food and fresh water. At a good guess, we were six days off our course and short of everything, so there was really no great choice in the matter. If there had been another way I would have chosen it in a moment, for this whole business was not to my liking. Becalmed, and swept far from the shores of Kenyarsha to be discovered most fortuitously by flying creatures. This, just as a fine wind lifts from the south. I could have put all that aside except for the words of Rhaiz:

"It has been written that you would come. Now, you are here."

I am not overly fond of prophecies. I know that such things are possible, but I do not care to hear about them—particularly if they concern me. I also know that I am sometimes guided on my path, but I prefer not to think about that, either. I have learned that it doesn't help to wonder just when and where some helping hand is nudging you along.

85

Rhaiz informed me that his people were called the Avak-har, and their city named Avak. It is nearly impossible to describe this place, for it is like no other city I have seen. I knew at once that it was an ancient site, and I longed to see it close at hand. Avak is built at the mouth of a great river, and the waters there have long since swallowed its streets and byways. Now, it is a place of crumbling spires that thrust above the river like the boles of winter trees. It is ideally suited for the Avakhar, who make their homes in these dizzy heights, and have no use for markets, shops and alleyways.

As we sailed in the shadow of these towers, I noticed each was linked to the other by a network of walkways—high bridges of sticks and rope hung slack as jungle vines. To me, it seemed all the world like some lazy spider's web. Did the Avakhar perfer to walk at times, instead of fly?

No, Rhaiz said shortly, such things were not for the People. The Avakhar had no need of bridges. His beak clamped firmly shut, and he would say no more.

We would not be staying in the towers, it was explained, as they had not been built to accommodate groundlings. Instead, we were taken to the natural bank of the river, where thatched houses had been constructed for our use. Clearly, couriers had flown well ahead of the *Ahzir,* for all was in readiness when we arrived.

If anything, I would say the Avakhar were overly generous in their greeting. As we eased our ship to shore, a noise like thunder split the air, and the sky was suddenly black with flying creatures. Our crew near took to their arms before we saw this was meant to be the friendliest of gestures. Hundreds of the Avakhar circled the ship, screaming and squawk-ing and drumming their wings upon the wind. Some carried flutes and other musical instruments, which added to the din. Others hauled large baskets between them, which they show-ered upon us quite freely until the decks were covered with fruits of all kinds, and multi-colored blossoms.

Only one unfortunate incident marred these ceremonies. Since we were guests, we could do no more than smile, and understand that all peoples the world over do not share the same customs. For among the other items that fell to our decks were large quantities of excrement. A great deal of this landed on members of the crew, including Rhalgorn, who happened to be looking up at the wrong time. We later learned that the Avakhar release their bowels freely whenever it occurs to them, and that we had not been singled out for any special favors.

I do not think Rhalgorn ever truly believed this. When he would speak to us again, he pointed out that he was grateful to be included in a venture that had discovered two distinct races that shared the same charming habit. Signar did his best to keep from laughing, and solemnly told the Stygiann we could at least be grateful the Kenyashii couldn't fly.

Squashed fruit, excrement and flower petals were boot deep upon our decks, and the *Ahzir* looked remarkably like a garbage scow. If I have learned anything in my travels, it is that fame and honor frequently come in strange packages.

In spite of the apparent friendliness of these people, we left a partial crew aboard our vessel. Rhaiz wondered at this, but I told him the relics of our gods were aboard, and demanded constant attention. The Avakhar are a religious folk, and he understood the importance of this.

"You can talk all you like about what a fine bunch of fellows they are," Signar said later, when we'd had our fill of fruits, breads and nuts, "but if we'd been *wrong* this afternoon and they'd come at us like that with weapons, we'd be most of us good and dead by now!"

He was right, of course, but we were much too weary to concern ourselves with what might have happened, and didn't. Still, we set up shifts for a watch, and kept our eyes open. We slept well, except for occasional bouts with lice, kindly left behind by our hosts.

There was more fruit in the morning, much to Rhalgorn's disgust. He showed his teeth and suggested that a good roast *bird* would be just the thing for breakfast.

Rhaiz appeared to show us his city, and we all accompanied him—even Lady Corysia, to my surprise. Signar said he had to see about provisions, and when Rhaiz assured him that would be taken care of, the Vikonen paled at the thought, and fled to the *Ahzir*.

A small flat boat took us from shore to the nearest of the towers. The creature who poled us across was fatter than the Avakhar I had seen, and stooped at the shoulders. His crest was nearly gone, and his feathers looked damp and sticky. When I gazed his way, he turned and hid his face. Rhaiz pretended not to notice he was there.

"You will only have to climb a short way up the face of the tower," he explained, "until we reach the first of the bridges. From there, one may easily cross to any point about the city."

Like all tourists, we followed his directions, mounting the crude stone steps to the landing. Beside me, Corysia turned ashen. The bridge stretched up to a far tower, until it seemed no thicker than a thread.

"Aldair, this will be suitable?" asked Rhaiz.

"Oh, yes, just fine," I told him. Corysia gave me a sharp, cutting glance. "What would you have me do," I asked, when we were out of the Avakhar's hearing, "tell him we're delicate creatures and too frightened to climb about on strings?"

"Why not? It's true, isn't it?"

"Yes, but what's that got to do with anything?"

"I only hope I live through this venture," she said darkly. "Nothing would give me greater pleasure than to introduce you to my uncle."

"I am sure Emperor Augustus is a delightful person, if he is a member of your family."

"He is. But I doubt that *you* would think so."

The Avakhar wheeled about the skies, gliding from one high perch to another, performing whatever business is important to people with wings. In truth, it was difficult to guess just what this business might be. Wherever we went we were greeted warmly and hailed as long-lost friends—but there was no sign that anyone was engaged in any sort of activity save flying. They gathered upon the dizzy heights and chattered among themselves, or climbed in and out of the thousands of stone caves that dotted the towers. Or—flew some more.

We did learn what the chubby, stooped members of the race were for, and why the bridges existed at all. They were land-bound Avakhar and no better than slaves. They carried fruits and nuts and other foods from the forest by the river, hauling them up the bridges from tower to tower. In a sense, I suppose they were no more miserable than slaves the world over. Still, their state seemed all the more pathetic, for they had known the soaring freedom of the skies.

The Niciean spotted the reason for this condition—a tendon slashed just behind the shoulder, where the great wings joined the body. "I am not overly impressed by the outward kindliness of these people," he whispered. "If they would do this to their own—"

Rhalgorn cut him off. "From what I have seen, they are

neither better nor worse than any other race—excluding the Stygianns, of course."

Thareesh glared at him and hissed beneath his breath. Rhalgorn only laughed. And there was little that either Thareesh or I could say, for the Stygiann was right. The Lords of the Lauvectii are a cruel and ruthless lot, to be sure —but they are the only creatures I know who never turn upon their own.

At the peak of the third high tower, Rhaiz stopped abruptly and turned his golden eyes upon me. "Here, Aldair, we must leave you for a while. Another will see that you join us below."

"What's that?" Rhalgorn moved up beside me.

Rhaiz laughed easily and shook his head. "Please. No harm will come to you among the Avakhar. Your companions need have no fear."

"His companions have no fear about them, friend," Rhalgorn said darkly. "That doesn't mean that they are fools." Thareesh nodded assent.

"Wait," I said. "What's this all about, Rhaiz?"

"It is Rhamil, Aldair. He would speak with you."

"And who's Rhamil? Your leader?"

"He is—Rhamil."

"That doesn't tell me much, does it?"

Rhaiz blinked. "Then I will tell you that he is the one I spoke of, aboard your vessel. The one who has long awaited your coming."

SEVENTEEN

As I mentioned later to Rhalgorn and Thareesh, the Avakhar would not have to employ a great deal of trickery, if they wished to do us in. "Why lure one of us from the rest, when they could simply get us *all* in the middle of one of those bridges, fly away, and loose the thing at one end?"

Rhalgorn's jaw fell. "I had really not considered that."

"Nor had I," added Thareesh.

"To be perfectly honest about it," I said, "neither had I, until this moment. Undoubtedly, we will remember it the next time we are up there."

Even though I was most curious about this Rhamil, I came close to ending that venture before it began. One step into his lair was enough to gag a Stygiann. This malodorous mixture was born of excrement, rotting fruit, bad breath and Creator knows what. Ruling all these varied smells was the overpowering scent of unwashed flesh.

"Ah, Aldair, come in, come in!" A torch thrust out of the darkness. On the other end was something I assumed was an Avakhar. Rhamil possessed none of the characteristics which lend these people grace and beauty. Golden eyes had turned a pallid yellow, and his once proud crest was worn to stubby quills. Indeed, he had few feathers left at all, and these seemed to detach themselves and flutter away before my eyes, leaving gray and mottled skin over fragile bones.

"Well, find yourself a place," he muttered, waddling off ahead. "There—no, there, I think. Damnable stool here somewhere." Wherever his fingers touched, a great cloud of dust took flight, setting me to fits of coughing.

Rhamil's quarters were as bizarre as its occupant. Stacks and bales of every sort of debris rose to the ceiling. Countless jars and pots of all sizes were strewn about on shelves, boxes, stools, kegs and barrels. Over the years, most of these vessels had been cracked or broken, and now lay in thick, hardened puddles of many smells and colors. There were bits and pieces of leaves, stones, seeds, feathers and glass. Drips, spatters, spills and scraps.

Still, a familiar chill touched the back of my neck, for behind this odorous litter I could see traces of the original walls —the smooth gray false-stone made by Man.

Rhamil seemed to follow my gaze. "Ah, you are truly *Dha'ir Tayamanda*, the one who will come." His old eyes flashed. "I see this clearly!"

"This is not something I greatly understand," I said. "I would be grateful if you told me what you are talking about."

"Ah, but you *know* that. It is in your eyes."

"Nevertheless, I would appreciate hearing it from you, for I have never heard of this—one who comes, or whatever."

Rhamil held up a finger. "Aldair, you need not play games with me."

"I am not, I assure you."

"We can trust one another."

"I'm sure this is true. Still—"

"Look, now," he said shortly, "you *are Dha'ir Tayamanda*. Don't try to get out of it. I have seen this, and it is so!" He muttered darkly to himself, pawing about among his litter, now and then glaring suspiciously at me. "Here," he said finally, flinging a dirty leather bag between us. "Pick a rock— any rock. Mix them up first. Take one out and don't show it to me."

"What for?"

"Damn me, can't you just do something, without asking questions?"

I did as he asked.

"It has the mark of the sun, does it not?"

"No."

"Wait—a crescent."

"No."

"Well what, then?"

"You want me to tell you?"

"Yes, yes, I said so, didn't I?"

"It is a star."

"Ah, of course."

"Of course what?"

"A star guides you. It is the sailor's stone. Your favorite colors are red and blue and you were born in the two-month. Your lucky number is 9. You have ventured far on a long voyage. This is so, is it not?"

"It is true that I am a sailor, and I think it is equally clear that I have ventured far. My clan colors are red and blue, as you can see from my tunic. I was born in the eight-month and not the second and I have no idea whether 9 is lucky for me or not."

Rhamil gave me a knowing smile. "But you're not *sure* it isn't, are you?"

"No, I am not," I said, fast losing patience with all this, "but I am just as certain you are not sure that it is, if you'll pardon me for saying so."

Rhamil shrugged, picking at his sparse feathers. Even in the feeble light I could see that his flesh was crawling with small mites. As I watched, he caught one of these, absently cracked it wtih his beak, and ate it. My stomach gave a turn. "I—think I should be getting back, now," I said, moving to my feet. "Thank you for your time."

"Certainly," Rhamil muttered, "whatever you like, Aldair. Incidentally, who is this *lort thairn?* He is much on your mind, I see."

"What?" I sat again. "Lord Tharrin—what do you know of Lord Tharrin?"

Rhamil grinned smugly. "You are most impolite, Aldair, not at all what I would expect in the *Dha'ir Tayamanda.* But one cannot alter the course of destiny."

"Look, you spoke of Lord Tharrin."

"Did I?"

"Yes, you did!"

"Oh. Well, what of it? Do you wish to know his lucky number? It is 4."

I took a deep breath. "Somehow, I cannot believe the Lord Tharrin has a lucky number."

"Of course he does. Everyone has a lucky number."

"And what else do you know, concerning the Lord Tharrin?"

Rhamil closed his eyes. "He is thinking of you, and sends you greetings. He says—"

"I don't think the Lord Tharrin is telling me *anything.*"

Rhamil looked disappointed. "You don't?"

"No."

"Well, perhaps not. You can't always tell about these things. At any rate, it is true that he would be much intrigued with the towers of the Avakhar, as he has a great love of ancient places."

I tried not to stare, but Rhamil was most adept at reading even the slightest change of expression. His rheumy eyes glowed with delight. "This has meaning for you, then. I thought as much."

"It—does," I admitted. Leaning closer, I studied him carefully. "Rhamil, what do you know about this place? *Who built the structures of the Avakhar—and when?*"

Rhamil sat back, running his fingers over one another. "I *knew* you were the *Dha'ir Tayamanda.* Didn't I tell you? Of course I know the age of the towers, Aldair. And who built them. I am a prophet of the Avakhar, and it is my business to know things."

"Who, then?"

"Who what?"

"Who *built* the towers!"

Rhamil winked. "Why, don't *you* know, Aldair?"

"I—yes, I do. Do you, or do you not?"

"Of course."

"Tell me, then."

"You tell me first."

"Look—"

"Please—" Rhamil raised a bony hand, then pressed it to his eyes. "It is very tiring to perform these marvels, Aldair. I will reveal other secrets tomorrow. Now, I must rest."

"You will—" I stood, sending pots and jars clattering. "*What* marvels, Rhamil? You have told me one thing that has truth in it. The rest is nonsense!"

Rhamil opened his eyes and picked another mite from under his wing. "I had intended to give you a new lucky number," he sniffed. "Now, you may not get it at all."

EIGHTEEN

A true gift of prophecy is exceedingly rare in this world, but there has never been a lack of rogues and charlatans. Most of these fellows have all the wisdom and insight of a radish, and some can not even predict where they will spend the night, or bed their next meal. Then, there are others who possess true powers, but cannot discern them from their own low gullery. I am certain Rhamil was among the latter. None of us had mentioned the Lord Tharrin, or his interest in antiquities. Still, Rhamil had seen him clearly—plucking him from Creator knows where amid a muddle of wrong birthdays and lucky numbers.

"He does not know the truth when he chokes on it," I said at supper. "But there is no denying he has a talent."

The others agreed, for it seems there is no land without its seers, both real and imagined. For the most part, they are harmless enough, and add charm to the marketplace. It is only when they achieve high religious office that they become irritating and dangerous.

Rhalgorn and Thareesh had much of interest to report from their own ventures. "This is a peculiar place indeed," said the Nicean. "At every hole we passed, we asked Rhaiz what its occupant might be doing there. It soon became obvious our guide had no idea what we were talking about. The words *merchant, craftsman* or *warrior* meant nothing to him. Aldair, they do not *have* occupations, as such. They neither build things nor trade with one another. They have no system of exchange such as coins or gems. What little work is done, is done by slaves."

"I saw a few bits of furniture and such in Rhamil's quarters."

"Perhaps. But the Avakhar did not make them. They found them here or got them somewhere else."

"They have to do *some*thing," I said, "besides fly."

"They do," Rhalgorn put in. "Show him your fine toys, Thareesh."

The Niciean brought something from his carrying pouch and laid it out on the mat between us. The objects he showed me seemed nothing more than short sticks the size of my fingers. There were a dozen or so, and each looked as if it had been chewed upon by some sort of insect.

"Not insects," Thareesh corrected. "The Avakhar themselves. We saw many creatures chewing upon these things, and Rhaiz explained that his people do not write with their hands—he was appalled to find that other races do. Instead, they inscribe some sort of characters upon these sticks with their beaks."

"That is a most unusual custom," I told the Niciean, "but it does not prove the Avakhar do nothing else. It is inconceivable to me that chewing bits of wood could occupy an entire civilization."

Thareesh turned his lidless eyes upon me. "I cannot read these scratchings, Aldair, but I have set a few to paper as they were told to me." Once again, he dipped into his pouch, and withdrew a bit of parchment in the spidery Niciean script:

> *"I have calculated that it would take 47 days to fly to the moon, but I may be wrong."*

> *"A person who suffers from burning feet can find relief in a mix of two parts powdered clove to a bowl of river mud."*

> *"I greet each day with a smile, but it does not take long to realize that I am merely repeating another yesterday. Sometimes I think I will simply quit smiling and see if anything happens."*

> *"How many ants would have to break wind simultaneously before anyone noticed?"*

"A person who talks too much gets a dry mouth and cannot spit as well as someone who is quiet all the time."

"I once found 417 seeds in a rhapayee fruit. The next day, I found one with no seeds at all."

"I have always wondered whether lice snore when they sleep."

Thareesh looked up and laid his papers aside. "You see? We are dealing with a race of amateur philosophers."

"Amateur is surely the word," I agreed. "I do not see anything here the world can't do without."

Rhalgorn scratched his nose. "I rather liked the one about the ants. It is something that never occurred to me."

In the late evening, I stood on the bank of the river, Thareesh beside me, and watched the sun fade behind clouds the color of fire. Our ship rode easily near the shore. Signar had worked hard at our repairs and provisioning, and we would be ready to sail at the end of another day. He had little use for the Avakhar, though much of this feeling was colored by the rather messy greeting we received upon our arrival. For once, both he and Rhalgorn were of the same mind.

I thought I saw Corysia on the decks, but could not be certain. After our breathless tour of the towers she had fled to the ship, swearing she would not set foot here again. It was cooler ashore, and of course I was to blame for depriving her of this comfort. Such a lovely, insufferable creature, I mused.

"Your thoughts are far away," said Thareesh.

"Much closer than you think, friend." He did not pursue this, for which I was grateful.

We watched encroaching darkness shade the high towers of the Avakhar, and followed great flights of the creatures winging their way to rocky perches for the night. "You will forgive me," I said, "if I find it difficult to let myself imagine that a race capable of soaring the skies thinks of nothing more meaningful than ant farts. As Rhalgorn would say, that is most unseemly."

"They also crack lice with their beaks," he said soberly, "and assign lucky numbers."

"And drop fruits and excrement upon visiting seamen."

We laughed together at these follies, and shook our heads in wonder.

"Damn me," I said, kicking a large stone down the hillside. "They have to be more than that, Thareesh. Don't they?"

"Why, because they perch atop the ruins of Man? A fool can live in ignorance amid the treasures of the world, Aldair."

I had to laugh at that. "Perhaps your words describe me, as well as the Avakhar." Thareesh gave me a questioning glance. "There are times, friend, when I feel most inadequate at this. I'm a warrior, not a scholar. We need the likes of a Fabius Domitius on this venture. I don't even know what I am looking for. More than that, I may not know it when I see it. Suppose there was something of importance in this very place. Would I know it?"

Thareesh smiled. "Even if we are not scholars, Aldair, we will surely know the place of Man when we come to it."

"Perhaps," I said. "If indeed we come to it at all."

"Do you believe that, truly?" The Niciean touched me gently. "I do not imagine that this seer of yours has brought you through so many wonders for nothing. It does not seem likely that he would do so, Aldair."

At that moment, his words meant little to me, for I doubted all that smacked of prophets and secrets and great quests after nothing. "Thareesh," I said, "I have despaired of this task of ours more than once. At times, I doubt that I am guided at all. At others, I am certain it is I who am too blind to see the proper path. I have even imagined that I dreamed it all—that there is no deep and hidden mystery to the world."

"And did you dream of Albion, too?" he asked. I didn't answer. Instead, I gazed up once again at the high towers of the Avakhar, near shrouded now in darkness.

Before I turned away from the shore, my eye caught a stir of movement near the bow of the *Ahzir*. Peering closer, I saw the great hulk of Juumb'ar, squatting alone in the shallows of the river. While I watched, he dipped his long, wormlike nose below the surface, filled it with water, and sprayed it over his shoulders. I watched him repeat this again and again, then finally followed Thareesh to our quarters.

Once more I was touched by the great sorrow of this creature. Like the slave who finally throws aside his collar of iron, the Kenyashii did not know what to do with his freedom.

He could neither go backward nor forward. He was bound forever in some frightening in-between.

And if, for a moment, I had doubted my quest, or the very real and terrible heritage of Man, Juumb'ar was enough to bring me to my senses.

NINETEEN

"Ah, Aldair, you are here. The stones foretold your coming!"

He sat where I had left him, amid the stench and clutter of his lair. No doubt, I was expected to pretend that he had not moved from this spot since the day before, or that I had not caught him peeking at me as I climbed the bridge.

"It is well that you have come," he said, blinking at the dark ceiling, "the signs are most auspicious for those born upon the two-month."

"Eight-month. And I did not climb up here for a lucky number, Rhamil. Yesterday, you spoke the name of a person most dear to me. More than that, Lord Tharrin was much a part of events which are of great import to myself and my companions. If you see more of these events within your stones, I—"

Rhamil waved me quiet and shook his head shortly. "You are brash and impertinent, Aldair. I am not sure you are ready to receive great secrets." He glared fiercely over his beak. "Don't think I don't *know* plenty, too."

"No impertinence was intended," I assured him. "Impatience, perhaps—"

"Youth and foolishness is what it is!" he snapped. Suddenly, he closed his eyes and touched his brow. "There is a loved one, far away. A mother—perhaps a sister?"

"Rhamil. Yesterday we talked about the towers of the Avakhar. You said you knew how old they were, and who built them. This is a part of the knowledge I seek."

"Indeed it is, Aldair. And well you should."

"What?"

"The truth is," he cleared his throat, "the towers are—old beyond counting. Yes, at least. And I—fear that I am not at liberty to reveal their maker."

"You are not at liberty, because you don't know!"

"I *do*, too!" he cried. His old eyes blazed. "You have no right to talk to me in that manner. I am a prophet of the Avakhar, which is a *race* of prophets, in case you didn't know. There is little worth *knowing* on this earth that I don't know or can't find out!"

"Except who built the towers," I reminded him.

He stared at me, trembling so hard his feathers began to fall like snow in the Northland. "You don't think so, do you? Well, come with me, Master Aldair, and I'll show you who built the towers—and other things as well!"

My heart fair leaped at once. Whether the old faker knew it or not, he would lead me to new understanding of the world of Man. Surely, new wonders awaited me below.

I followed him through the rear of his cave past a narrow doorway I had missed before. He led us down a long, treacherous spiral of dust and rubble, dragging his wings behind him. In the light of his guttering torch I could see great slabs of Man-stone on every side, veined with strands of rust. While I have seen such things before, it is easy to forget how lavishly Man used the metals of the earth. He can be despised for his treachery, but there is no denying his greatness.

A column of cool, damp air rose from the depths, carrying the unmistakable odor of the Avakhar. The lower we descended, the worse this stench became, until I was certain half the race must be quartered below.

Now, more torches could be seen, and it was clear we were coming to the end of our climb. Quite suddenly, a great room opened up beneath us. Squinting, I could make out someone —or something—moving about. Rhamil turned, his eyes bright. "Aldair—I perceive you have a brother. His name is Reep, is it not?"

"Rheif," I said, somewhat astounded at this new bit of truth he had pulled out of the ether. "And he is, or was, a brother in every way, though we—*Creator's Eyes, what in all the hells is that!*"

Rhamil grinned happily, stepping aside so I could see. "I told you, didn't I, that I would show you great wonders? Well, there you are!"

"Yes, but—what is it?"

The longer I stared at the thing, the less I understood. It was a large spoked wheel, lying parallel, and somehow connected, to the Man-stone floor beneath. A dozen slaves turned the wheel at a slow, leaden pace, while Avakhar guards looked on.

The real marvel, though, was perched atop the wheel itself. A wooden pole rose from its center, and from this pole jutted hundreds of sharp little bony spikes. Stuck to each spike was something I suddenly realized I had seen before— those peculiar wooden sticks the Avakhar inscribe with such wisdom as the number of seeds in a fruit, and the snoring habits of lice.

"Well," asked Rhamil, "what do you think?"

"I am afraid," I said honestly, "it passes understanding."

"No doubt. It is the habit of those who lack true knowledge to belittle their betters, Aldair. You speak, but say nothing. You look, but cannot see." He spread one spindly arm to take in the scene before us. "There, Master Skeptic, is the answer to your questions. Who built the towers of the Avakhar? The Creator himself, of course. And how old might they be? The word does not apply, for they have been here forever."

"What?"

"Of course!"

"But—Rhamil, what is it? What does it *do?*"

Rhamil looked pained. "Aldair, what it *does* is *create*, for this very room is the *seat of creation*. The thoughts of the Avakhar are placed upon this pole, where their meaning is absorbed by the Universal Fluid. The thoughts are changed each day, and new ones added. At some future time, no one can say exactly when, all possible thoughts will have been placed upon the pole and absorbed. Then, the world will be created, and all its creatures born."

"Born?"

"I know," he smiled patiently, "so much understanding in one day has shaken you considerably. From listening to you and your companions, we realize you suffer from the delusion that you are alive. This is not true, of course. We are all, as yet, unborn. We only *dream* of reality. Obviously, there can be no life until all thought is absorbed by the Universal Fluid, for thoughts are the building stones which bind the cosmos together."

Thus, seeking the secrets of Man, I stumbled upon the

keys to the universe, which are little sticks gnawed by the
Avakhar. I am in no position to criticize the Creator, but if I
were asked I would say the one thing he could have easily
left out of his works is religion. From what I have seen, it
does more harm than good, and has little to do with the
Creator himself.

Having seen everything, there is little else to see. I followed Rhamil back through the bowels of the tower, up the
long spiral of debris. This time, I carried a torch of my own,
and I could see there was more than crumbled Man-stone
lying about. Bits of glass and crockery, ground by the ages.
Occasional splinters of wire turned green and brittle. I could
not even guess what many of the tiny shards I examined were
made of.

Lord Tharrin would have given an arm to see this place!
All he had known of antiquity was the flat and sterile ruin of
Tarconii. And I, who could not touch his knowledge, had
climbed the towers of the Avakhar—and walked the halls of
Albion. One of us had seen too little. The other, far too much.

Something caught my torch. I stopped, leaned down to
scrape small rocks aside, and brought the thing to better light.
It was a small sphere, no bigger than an egg. Smooth, like
glass, but of a different substance. Wetting a finger, I wiped
the dust of centuries aside and studied it closely. Though
part of the object was worn and damaged, I could still trace
a pattern with my fingers. Lines, running evenly around its
surface. Other lines, at angles to those.

The sudden realization of what I was seeing nearly turned
my legs to water. There, the coast of Gaullia, and what must
be Island Albion. Below, the bulge of Tarconii, the Southern
Sea, and the unmistakable boot of Rhemia. Across from that,
the desert lands of Niciea, and the whole vast continent of
Kenyarsha. It had to be, though no living creature had
charted its shores.

My heart pounded against my chest. Why would the race
of Man wrap charts about a sphere, *unless that was the shape
of the world?* Could such a thing be so? And if a ship did *not*
fall off into the Great Emptiness, but simply kept on going—

The small thing trembled in my hand. Out beyond Albion,
past the Misty Sea, two great continents ranged north and
south, held by a narrow thread of land. And beyond that—

Loud shouts of anger brought me up fast. Torches lit the
darkness and there were suddenly Avakhar all around me,

waddling down the slope as fast as their awkward legs could carry them. It may be there were no true warriors in this society, as Thareesh believed, but these had found some wicked pointed sticks to wave in my direction.

TWENTY

At such times, it us unwise to stop and ask questions. Creatures with weapons are seldom in the mood to explain their actions. Thus, I gave them some action of my own, matching them yell for yell, and whirling my sword about in fancy circles. As I guessed, the Avakhar were proficient at shrieking and hopping about, but knew little about fighting. The first wooden stick I hewed in half sent them squawking for cover, beating their wings against the dust. Somewhere along the way I passed Rhamil, but did not stop to chat.

Outside, I paused, squinting against the sun. This is not good strategy against flying things. Wings drummed above and a shadow covered my tracks. I ducked for cover, but an Avakhar sent me sprawling. There were hundreds of them, circling the tower. I couldn't imagine what had stirred them to such activity, but this was clearly no place to find out. The air is the element of the Avakhar, and the ground is mine. Without glancing up or below, I started off fast across the bridge, praying some fool would not decide to slash it, with me in the middle.

The Avakhar left me alone; content, now, to screech about and make the bridge sway fearfully. Reaching the second tower safely, I started down for the third. Rhalgorn met me, waving his sword and snarling at the Avakhar, daring them to come a feather closer.

"There appears to be some problem," I said.

"There is, but I suggest we get down from this thing first. It is not a seemly place to talk."

A chaotic scene awaited us below. A dozen crewmen were backed against the base of the tower, brandishing their weapons. Thareesh stood at their point, his curved Niciean bow drawn to the ready. Surrounding this group were more Avakhar than I cared to count. They milled about like angry bees, sending their raucous cries to the sky.

"It is something to do with that damnable Kenyashii," Rhalgorn shouted above the din. "That's all I've been able to make out. They have him over there, near the shore!"

I looked where he pointed, but could see nothing but Avakhar. Beyond, the flying creatures hovered about our ship, swooping and shrieking and making a general nuisance of themselves. Signar, of course, had the sense to keep the rest of the crew aboard. If we needed help, it would come.

I spotted Rhaiz just outside our circle, and pushed my way to him. "If you will quiet your people," I yelled, "we can see what this is about. This racket will accomplish nothing!"

He glared at me, anger in his golden eyes—but he held up a hand and brought his people to a stop. There was still a great deal of squawking and clicking of beaks, but we could hear one another.

"Whatever you wish to say, say it quickly," he told me. "The Avakhar are angry, and I do not expect I can hold them back forever."

"It would be well if you did," I warned him, "for my crew will use their weapons if they have to. They have restrained themselves admirably, under the circumstances. It would be best if you simply told me what this is about."

"What—" Rhaiz took a breath and swallowed his anger. "What it is *about*, Aldair, is that great lumbering thing over there. I don't know what it is called and don't care to. He has desecrated sacred ground, a thing that is intolerable to the Avakhar!"

"He has what? What exactly did he desecrate?"

"The *chelah*, to be exact. It is the burial ground of the Avakhar." Having said this, he took a moment to shudder. "I do not even wish to speak of this, but I suppose I must."

"I think that would be a good idea, otherwise we will never get to the end of it. What—*how* did Juumb'ar do this thing?"

"He relieved himself upon it," snapped Rhaiz, "that's how!"

"He did?"

"He most certainly did!"

It seemed most ironic that the one trait the Kenyashii and the Avakhar seemed to share—defecating on everything in sight—should be a sin of any sort. Still, after my visit to the seat of creation, I suppose I should not have been surprised at anything I saw among those people.

"I am greatly sorry this happened," I told him, "and I am certain the poor fellow had no idea what he was doing. He seldom does."

"His intentions have little to do with the matter. What's done is done."

"—And cannot be undone," I reminded him, becoming more than a little weary of Avakhar spiritual matters. "As far as this *sin* is concerned, Rhaiz, it occurs to me that it would be difficult to desecrate the burial ground of the Avakhar. If all creatures upon the earth are yet unborn, there can hardly be dead to bury—there is no one alive to die. I find this hard to understand."

Rhaiz gave me a withering stare. "I am not surprised, since you are not of the Avakhar, and ignorant of the Creator's plan. I did not say those interred in the *chelah* were dead. That is your word, not ours. Every child knows there comes a time when people stop breathing. We do not know why this is so, but it happens. Certainly, as you yourself pointed out, it has nothing to do with death, which is not possible until the world begins. Nevertheless, creatures who no longer move about become stiff, and useless, and smell a great deal. Thus, it is necessary to confine them to the *chelah*."

I did not comment upon this. I simply thanked him politely, and said that I appreciated the explanation. "And again, Rhaiz, I apologize to the Avakhar. We deeply regret that this has happened."

"It goes without saying that your apology is not accepted," he said stiffly. "It would be best if your people left the shores of Indrae as soon as possible. The Avakhar can no longer welcome you here."

"I'll see to it at once," I told him, and turned to Rhalgorn.

"The offender, of course, must stay."

"What?" I jerked around and faced him. "Now just a minute—!"

Rhaiz stopped me. "Aldair, you must listen to what I say. This offense cannot go unpunished. It has happened, and no words can take it away. I know it is in your mind to defy us. I also know that the Avakhar have no weapons to match your own. We are not a warlike people—but we will fight to protect our beliefs. You can do much damage here, but there are more of my people than yours. In the end, many creatures will lie still upon the ground, without breath or movement. Some of them will not be of the Avakhar."

There was no more anger in his voice, only sober determination. Those harsh golden eyes assured me he was ready to carry out this foolishness to the limit.

"Rhaiz, I cannot allow you to harm this creature," I told him. "He does not even know what he has done."

Rhaiz looked surprised. "Aldair, I did not say that we would *harm* him."

"No, but—"

"I said that he must be *punished*. Punishment is not the task of the unborn; it is the province of the Creator. He will merely be sent from here," he pointed north, "to the Great Wastes."

"And what happens to him there?"

"Nothing. It is barren, and devoid of all things. There is nothing there to harm him."

I laughed aloud. "Or help him, either, I'd imagine. You mix your words nicely, Rhaiz. He'll not be hurt. He'll just die."

"You are mistaken," Rhaiz said solemnly. "Nothing can die that is yet unborn."

I could not let them do that to Juumb'ar. Whatever he was, he was a living creature, and he deserved a better chance than no chance at all. "Then I will go with him to this place," I said. "He is much too foolish to travel alone."

"Aldair," Rhalgorn's eyes went wide, "have you lost your senses?"

Rhaiz looked at me a long moment, nodded, and turned away.

"This is plain foolishness," growled the Stygiann. "That great tub of lard is not worth a life, Aldair. He has plagued us since the start of this venture, and if the god of the Avakhar wishes to have him, I, for one, will be pleased to let him go."

"Rhalgorn," I grinned, "this sudden spiritual awakening of yours is most becoming."

"It is better than dying—a state which is quite possible among my people, as well as your own."

"I have no intention of finding out," I explained. "If it will satisfy the Avakhar and avoid a fight, I'll go along with Juumb'ar to these Wastes, whatever they may be. Tell Signar to follow the coast north. I'll cut west as soon as we're out of sight of the Avakhar, and join you."

Rhalgorn looked wary. "It sounds easy enough. Things always do, I notice, until you do them." He was more than right in this, though I had no way of knowing at the time.

~~~~~~~~~~~~~~~

TWENTY-ONE

~~~~~~~~~~~~~~~

As I watched my companions sail from Indrae, I realized what a fool I had been to trust these people. The Avakhar could be struck by new spiritual insight at any moment, and devise some entirely different form of punishment for Juumb'ar—something, perhaps, that entailed the dropping of great weights into a river. All things are possible for a race that fills its graves with the yet unborn.

As it happened, they were true to their word—most likely, because there was no need to create a greater form of misery than the Wastes.

Without ceremony, we were taken a few leagues north of the river, through heavy forest as dense as any I had seen in Kenyarsha. At the end of this growth, however, the trees gave way abruptly, and we came out upon a bleak, barren plain, baked by a copper sun.

My heart dropped at the sight. Beside me, Juumb'ar whimpered and rolled his eyes in fear. I have known the Great Desert below Chaarduz, where Thareesh and I nearly lost our lives against the legions of Fhazir. It is a fearsome place, for sure. At the moment, though, I remembered it almost fondly. Here, the very earth seemed afire, like the face of the sun. The ground beneath our feet was raw and red, covered with shards of brittle stone that burned right through my boots. The air was hot and still, and thick as syrup.

It was here the Avakhar left us. Rhaiz simply pointed north toward nothing, and disappeared beneath the trees with his

companions. I was sure, though, they watched to see we kept
our course.

"We had best be going," I told Juumb'ar. "There is a
rather long walk ahead."

Juumb'ar trembled all over. "We can't be *goesing* out
there," he squealed. "Wes no getting foods or waters, Aldair!"

"We'll get food and water when we reach the ship. It won't
be long. You'll just have to go without for the moment."

The Kenyashii stuck his nose in his mouth and wailed, re-
fusing to budge. However, when I turned and walked away
he found new strength, and was soon shuffling along behind.

A person can die rather quickly in the desert. Without
proper clothing, such as the Niciean traveler wears, he fries
in the open sun. Without water, his body becomes as dry as a
stone within hours. Looking out upon that bleak and terrible
land, my words to Rhalgorn seemed hollow and empty. It
was fair enough to say we would simply turn westward to the
sea. Surely, it was no more than an easy day's march away.
Easy, if one is strolling the footpaths of Gaullia.

I did not count the number of times Juumb'ar collapsed
upon the earth to die. If it had not been well past the middle
of the day when we began that trek, he would have perished
for sure. This is not to say I enjoyed our venture, but there
is a great difference between the Kenyashii's approach to life,
and my own. He was already convinced that he would die,
and that is the first step in making it come true.

When the sun finally collapsed in a great pool of fire, we
sank gratefully to the ground, though the earth was still hot
enough to blister.

"We can stay here a moment," I told him. "No longer."

Juumb'ar said nothing. He simply stared past me with
empty eyes. Gray, parched skin hung in dry folds over his
enormous body. "No goesing wheres, Aldair," he said finally.
"Wants to drinking some *waters!*"

"That's *why* we can't stop," I explained. "We have to use
the night, Juumb'ar. The sea can't be far, now. We can reach
it before morning."

"Thems flying things bes coming to hurt us," he wailed.
"They will, Aldair!"

"No. Don't worry about them."

"They bes scaring me. They do. Wants some waters, Al-
dairs."

Surely, I thought, the Creator has saddled me with this great cumbersome child for some purpose. What was I *doing* in this place, baking my snout to the bone? Sooner or later, would something go *right* on this venture?

The terrible earth softened under twilight. Juumb'ar sat like an enormous lump of tallow, silent and unbreathing. If I left him there, I told myself, I could probably make it to the sea. If I stayed, there would surely be two dead wanderers in the Wastes before the sun set again.

Shifting on the hot ground, my weight pressed a hard stone into my leg and I reached down irritably to pluck it away. When I held it to the fading light, the milky surface of the little sphere winked back at me. As tired as I was, I felt a sudden chill of excitement. How could I think of giving up, when the whole world, with all its unknown lands, lay there in the palm of my hand?

I had no great interest in perishing in the Wastes, and would not, if I could help it. I would do the best I could with Juumb'ar. He would have to do the rest.

Everything hurt. Even a few moments rest had left me stiff from the day. Bracing my hands upon the ground, I stood up shakily. First one leg, then the other. Finally, I was there, both feet firmly on the earth. Rocky, perhaps, but—

Suddenly, my stomach turned, and the landscape swirled and melted around me. I felt my knees give way and saw the darkness pressing in. No, I told myself firmly, you are not allowed to pass out, Aldair. If you do, the night will speed away, and that is the one thing that will kill you for certain. . . .

TWENTY-TWO

The thing held me with its great thorny foot and laughed. I choked on mud at the bottom of a dark and smelly sea and this seemed to amuse the creature immensely. It rumbled and hooted and ground me deeper into the muck. I gasped for breath, and knew my lungs were busting. It read my fears like words in stone and laughed, and laughed, and laughed. . . .

My own dream-cries followed me out of sleep. Sitting abruptly, I stared into the night. The sight of darkness swept all false fears aside and filled me with real and solid alarm. How long had I slept? How many precious hours were already far behind me? At least, there were no pale streaks of morning in the sky—there was still some time before the killing sun came up to claim us.

"Juumb'ar, we— Juumb'ar?" Standing, I searched the land around me. *"Juumb'ar!"*

He was gone. I called again. But no answer came from the night. It would be fine and noble to say I searched far and wide for the Kenyashii, risking valuable minutes of darkness. In truth, though, I did nothing of the sort. If I'd thought there was a chance in a thousand of finding him, and herding him toward the sea, I would have taken that chance. I had gone this far, but I could go no further, and spend my life for nothing. I might make it to the sea if I tried for it now. If I did not, I would be lost. Even an hour under that sun would be ample time to kill me.

West, then, and the *Ahzir*. If I knew my companions at

112

all, they were already ashore there and waiting. Perhaps they had even struck off inland, to guide our way, so we— I stopped, and went cold all over. West? *Creator's Eyes, which way was west!*

The dark sky whirled about, dotted with a million unfamiliar stars. There was nothing in the night I knew, not one remembered constellation. Desperately, I searched the skies, trying to recall even one thing Signar had told me. Was that the cloak of The Miller, just above the horizon? If it was, it came from Northland skies, and the west was to my left. If I was wrong—

I laughed aloud. With the dawn, I would know my way for certain. Even a turnip feels the sun rise in the east!

Suddenly, sound cut through the night and set my hairs on end. I listened. In moments, it came again. "Juumb'ar!" I shouted, "here!" That pitiful wail was all too familiar. Turning, I made my way to it, as fast as weary legs could take me.

Next time, it was closer. "Juumb'ar!" Ahead, the land rose slightly, curving toward a small dry hillock. My boots slipped over the loose surface, sending dry stone rattling down behind. "Juumb'ar!" Then, I was at the crest and over—

—and just as quickly, clawing to get away, back to the other side. My hands raked earth, making furrows down the slope. I was falling. It was a long, terrible fall that took a million dusty years. The nightmare thing I could not see loped just behind me. I could smell its wetness, feel its awful hunger as it gnawed and ripped and tore me in its mind. . . .

Forever stopped. Dirt was in my mouth, stone against my cheek. I traced the stone with a finger, and followed it with my eyes. It stretched above me, a scratch against the sky. There were others, as far as I could see. Dark, square columns —some still tall above the ground, some only blunt and stubby fingers. I touched it again to be sure. But I already knew that it was Man-stone.

What sort of place had we stumbled upon, I wondered? I was not overly surprised to find a Man-place, for we were close enough to the towers of the Avakhar. No doubt, there was more than one site such as this around that ancient city. Only, this place had a special air about it. A terrible sense of desolation. As if something had begun, and ended abruptly.

There was probably a good reason for this, I decided. One that had little to do with the site itself. For I knew very well what had struck me as I came over that hill. Juumb'ar had discovered another of his damnable amulets. It could be nothing else but that. He could *smell* the things, like a horse after water. For the moment, the columns were shielding me from its power. But it was there. I could feel it at the back of my neck.

And that, of course, presented a greater problem: if he had the thing, how was I going to get it from him—and get us out of here before the sun came up and, caught us? I couldn't get near him, and if he came to me—

I looked about me. The columns. Darkness. Nothing. Then, something—a square, black shadow. Large, with smaller shadows scattered about. Carefully, I worked my way to it, keeping the columns well between myself and the place I guessed Juumb'ar to be. My fingers touched a flat, metal surface, scarred and pitted with age. Running my hand further, I found that the mass itself was no single object, but a stack of metal squares or boxes. Each box measured roughly half a meter, and the smaller objects I'd seen were boxes that had fallen from the pile.

At any other time, I would have been greatly interested in the artifacts of Man, whatever they might be. Now, I had but a single purpose in mind: get Juumb'ar away from his toy, and run like a hare to the sea. Perhaps my thoughts were too much on this problem, and not upon the moment. At any rate, I did a very foolish thing. As I crawled along behind my boxes, the stack suddenly ended—and I kept going.

The fear that had found me on the *Ahzir*, and again, only moments before, was no more than a gnat's kiss. I cannot begin to describe the thing that touched me, and will not even try. I am sure the awful surge of its power is what saved me, for it dealt me such a real and physical blow I staggered back and fell behind my boxes.

Instantly, it was gone. But what I saw there, I will not soon forget.

If the gods wished to mock me, this was clearly the time. I have been swept from my goal, and set upon strange seas around an unknown land. I have been plagued by storms, Rhemians and the Avakhar. I have been showered with excrement, and shunned by a royal maiden. Yet, none of these things have troubled me more than Juumb'ar the Kenyashii.

Once, in Silium, I saw some wag tie a fish to the leg of a fool. The poor fellow had no idea where the smell was coming from, so he dragged it with him everywhere. My fish is larger, and more odorous, but he is bound to me all the same. And I suppose there is some irony in this—that a large and bothersome lout should lead me to the thing I sailed clear to the ends of the earth to find.

In the few seconds I saw him there, I knew it was no mere amulet that held the Kenyashii. There were boxes, a pile like my own. Only some great force had swept across them, like a poker through a fine fat cheese. They lay all about, or what was left of them, in an ancient puddle of slag. Whatever had destroyed these things had left one untouched, or nearly so. The burning force had merely brushed the box with its power. There was a crack, no larger than a hair, and through that crack a faint red glimmer caught the night.

What awesome power was locked within that thing! The tiny eye of Juumb'ar's amulet had nearly destroyed us all, yet each of these dark cubes must hold a hundred-thousand times its power.

I could not guess why Man had raised these columns in the Wastes, and left them half completed. Or what had turned his metal stacks to butter. *I only knew for certain that the place I had seen in the windows under Albion did not lie in the desert below Niciea—but here, in the Great Waste itself. —That here, were the terrible devices that locked the gates of history, and made slaves of every creature.*

The stars wheeled about the heavens. Did I only imagine that a faint smudge of gray already touched the horizon? "Juumb'ar, listen! It's me, Aldair!"

Nothing. I was certain the sky was lighter. Even if we started now— "Juumb'ar, *answer* me!" A faint, almost imperceptible whimper. "Juumb'ar, you have to come out of there. *Now!*"

"No mores coming," he whined back, "it stayings *here,* Aldair."

"You can't stay here. If you do, you'll die. Do you know that, Juumb'ar?"

"Juumb'ar isn't bes dying!"

"You are, too. You will!"

A thought struck me. I moved a few paces from the pile. "Juumb'ar, I'm leaving now. I'm going to leave you *right here.* With no food or water. Do you understand that?"

He didn't, of course. The poor pitiful creature knew a greater hunger, now.

"All right," I shouted, "stay there, damn you! And you

know what? The *flying* things are coming. Right *now*. They're coming after *you*, Juumb'ar!"

A high, keening wail cut the night. It was a sound that surely carried all the fright and loneliness in the world.

—And then he came rumbling around that metal stack, shaking the earth beneath him. His tiny eyes were wide with fear; his nose made terrible noises, and his fan-like ears trembled like leaves in a storm. He waddled toward me fast as his legs would carry him, and when he was close enough, I saw how clever I had been to scare him into action—for he carried that deadly metal box clutched tightly in his stubby little arms.

~~~~~~~~~~~

TWENTY-THREE

~~~~~~~~~~~

If this be the Afterworld, I decided, it is truly worthy of its name. No fiery suns reached down to sear the flesh—only cool and soothing breezes brushed my skin. All about was bathed in rosy shadow, and touched with the breath of clove.

"Aldair?"

Something moved against that shadow—a friendly spirit come to greet me.

"Aldair—dearest Aldair, speak to me, please!"

Soft fingers touched me. Cool lips came down to mine and lingered there. If I had doubted where I was before, there could be no question now. I had ascended to Paradise—and then some. In addition to other comforts, the good Creator had provided me with a loving female. She was like Corysia in every way save one—for this heavenly creature neither scratched nor kicked nor screeched like an owl. Instead, she practiced all those arts one would expect to find in a better world.

The next time I awoke, neither the Afterworld nor Corysia's twin were about—only the broad, furry features of Signar-Haldring. "Ah, back among the living, are you?" A big grin creased his muzzle.

"Signar—where am I?"

A familiar snort came from behind the Vikonen. "Where am I, indeed," said Rhalgorn. "Hopefully, I will hear more original chatter before I leave this world."

"That will be sooner than you think," Signar growled, "if

you do not hold your Stygiann tongue. Aldair—we were truly worried for a time. The sun near ate you in that place. It's been three full days since we brought you back aboard. For a while—"

"Brought me—" I sat up abruptly, remembering. Pain hit me in a thousand different places. I dropped back, gasping for breath.

"Creator's Eyes," snapped Signar, "You mustn't move about like that. You're burned like a fine roast!"

"Signar, Rhalgorn—I *have* to know what happened out there! All I can recall is Juumb'ar—and—coming right at me with—with that Man-thing in his arms!"

Rhalgorn and Signar exchanged puzzled looks. "If you mean that peculiar box," said the Stygiann, "why, there's no cause to worry, Aldair. It's up on deck right now—Juumb'ar himself brought it safely aboard for you."

I stared, pulling myself up through pain and fighting friendly arms that held me back. Finally, nothing hurt at all anymore, and I sank gratefully into a dark and syrupy sea.

As strength and reason returned, I brought together the loose ends of events that had occurred without me. My companions didn't wait for us to reach them, but struck out quickly across the Wastes. There they found us, and clearly none too soon. Juumb'ar was still on his feet, wailing at the sun, and walking in the wrong direction. More surprising than that, he was carrying me across his shoulders. Why he bothered to take me with him, I cannot say. It was a wholly alien act for that pitiful creature. Never, at any time, had I seen him show compassion for another being.

Now, we would never know what possessed him during those moments, for he did not speak a word after his return to the *Ahzir*. Something happened to him out on the Wastes. The terrible power of the Man-thing destroyed his last semblance of will, and left him with no mind of his own. He would neither eat nor drink, and was totally unaware of our presence. There was nothing we could do for him, and finally, five days after we came out of the Wastes, Juumb'ar of the Kenyashii simply died.

It is hard to say what any of us felt about this creature. He caused us all much pain. He had no redeeming qualities to speak of, and made no friends aboard the *Ahzir*. How could one say, without shame, that he was missed or mourned?

Thareesh the Nicean expressed it better than any of us: "One can neither like nor loathe the being, Aldair, for there

was only emptiness within him. Still, this was not of his
doing, and I will not dishonor him with pity."

If Juumb'ar left anything of himself aboard the *Ahzir*,
it was a new and terrible hatred within us all for those long-
dead creatures who had stolen his soul.

Our mystery of the metal box was easily solved. When no
reasonable answers come to mind, one is forced to search
further afield. The Man-thing was clearly with us, squatting
ominously on the deck. Since it was there, and had not
destroyed us all, it was equally clear what had happened.
When I threatened him with the Avakhir, Juumb'ar did not
pick up the cube releasing its deadly emanations. Perhaps it
was fused to the pile of slag, and couldn't be removed. It's
as likely an answer as any. For better or worse, then, we had
a safer sample of the thing aboard.

When I told my companions all that had happened out
there, and my thoughts on this discovery, both Signar and
Rhalgorn were for tossing it overboard at once. When they
saw I disagreed, they stared as if I'd lost my senses.

"I cannot believe you've forgotten what happened on the
other side of Kenyarsha," Signar rumbled. "And from your
words, this is the great-great-grandfather of that damnable
amulet!"

"I have not forgotten," I told him. "I have also not forgotten what we came for, or why we risked our lives against
Rhemians, the sea, and a hundred other dangers. We
searched for such a thing—and now we have it. I will not
question how I came upon that place, or why a piece of it
followed me here. I only know that it has."

For a moment, I paused, and touched their eyes with mine.
It was evening, and pleasant winds urged us to the north.
Land appeared on either side, now—the bulk of Kenyarsha
to the west, and whatever shores lay to the east. Long ago,
Thareesh told me we might reach the east by sailing around
Kenyarsha. I have held within my fingers a small and perfect
model of the world, and seen those waters do indeed meet the
Southern Sea. I am certain, now, that I have glimpsed them
before, when Nhidaaj the Cygnian and I journeyed below
Xandropolis with the child-prince of the Niceans. There,
before I met the yellow-eyed seer in the desert, Nhidaaj
showed me the tips of great pyramids above the dark waters,
and told me they were near as old as anything on the Earth.

At the time, I did not know it was Man the great enemy himself who had built them.

I am sorry to say that small and ancient globe I found among the Avakhar is no longer in my hands. It lies somewhere behind us, on the baking stones of the Great Wastes. I regret this, for I would like to look at it again.

"None of us would deny the importance of our quest," Signar was saying. "There's not a creature who's heard the secret of Albion wouldn't lay down his life to do what must be done. But we'll do the world no favor goin' mad for it!"

"Signar," I said, "I do not believe this thing will drive us to madness. Whatever the thing is made of, it has held back the elements a hundred centuries or more. Reason tells me that as long as the metal encloses its power, we cannot suffer from it."

"Reason, indeed," sniffed Rhalgorn, shrugging his gaunt shoulders.

"What Aldair says is true," hissed Thareesh. "I have examined the thing, and though it is relatively simple to open—"

"Huh?" Rhalgorn's cup fell from his fingers.

"Please—". Thareesh held up a slim green hand. "I did not say I had opened it. Only that it was easily done. There are two simple catches on either side."

"Could this—happen accidentally?" I asked, as alarmed as Rhalgorn at this information.

"Not easily, though I suppose it could happen, if some great force were to strike it. I am surprised," he said wryly, glancing at Rhalgorn, "that you have not discovered this yourself, as Stygianns appear to have a great deal of curiosity about things that are locked or closed in any way."

Rhalgorn snarled at him, but said nothing.

"At any rate, make sure the thing's got a crewman around it at all times," I said. "I think it ought to be lashed securely, as well."

Signar gave me a solemn stare. "Which means we're going to keep the thing."

"It does."

"I put a viper under a bucket once," Rhalgorn announced. "It was safe enough until it burrowed out and got in bed with a cousin of mine. Fortunately, it was a somewhat distant cousin and we were not well acquainted."

"We are not dealing with vipers here," I told him.

"No, we are not, Aldair. And though I sense you find my

story foolish and unimportant, I would remind you there is some wisdom in it. If we are keeping this thing under its bucket, so to speak, I assume we have some reason for it."

I nodded, and came around to fill my cup. "It appears to me we have the key to two great secrets here. First, these cubes contain some power that induces fear, illusion—even madness. In a sense, gigantic amulets. They are also similar to those devices which isolated Albion, and kept Man's secret through the centuries. Maybe, though, they are more than that. Either these things or something very much like them have guided history since we were first set here and given life. They have served as both the sentinel and the whip of Man. We knew they existed. Now we know something more. This awesome power *can* be contained. Wherever these things are hidden about the Earth, they can be found, in time— and stopped. It is a deadly thing upon our deck, there. But we can learn to conquer it."

"Maybe," Rhalgorn said soberly. "We have a saying, though, in the Lauvectii. 'It is difficult to study vipers under buckets—and foolish to study them anywhere else.' "

"I do not believe there is such a saying in the Lauvectii," I told him, more than a little irritated.

"No," he admitted, "but there will be, if I ever see the place again."

TWENTY-FOUR

It was not a night for sleeping. More than once, I closed my eyes to wake again in some nightmare land. I dreamed a great viper crawled from that thing upon our deck and made its way below, seeking me out with green and shining eyes. I dreamed of Rhamil atop his high tower. "All the thoughts of the cosmos have now been perceived," he announced. "It is time for the world to begin, Aldair." As he spoke, creation burst upon us with a sad and lonely wail. I was born, from a small speckled egg, and when I saw what I had become—

Finally, I fled my quarters and made my way above, stopping to dash cold water in my face. Familiar northern stars now filled the sky ahead. The *Ahzir* cleaved the seas, laying clean white foam upon the water. I filled my lungs with salt-fresh air and listened to the night.

Perhaps it was the cool sea wind upon my sun-scorched hide, or the residue of dreams. Whatever the cause, I was overcome for a moment with a terrible sense of loneliness and sorrow. Tears blurred my eyes, and I longed to be away from that place, and back in the broad valleys of the Eubirones. I thought of the smells of the marketplace, and the colors of autumn. I saw the faces of my friends and family, as if they were there beside me. Even people I hardly knew seemed dear to me now. Real work was a joyous memory, and long, tiring days atop a wagon in the fields the most pleasant thing I could remember.

By dawn, most of this business had passed, and I felt

neither better nor worse than I had before. After a mug of
barley beer I joined the others on deck, and announced that
we would pass through the Southern Sea—Rhemians or no
Rhemians—and sail to Albion. There, we would deliver our
'bucket of vipers' to Fabius Domitius and the other scholars
toiling there. No one seemed overly surprised at this.

Late in the evening, the shore on either side began to
narrow considerably. Clusters of green palms appeared, and
flocks of snowy waterbirds. Signar wisely decided he did not
care to navigate these waters in the dark. He had just called
the order to drop anchor in midstream when the lookout
shouted that we had company—a dozen riders approaching
fast along the shores to port.

In seconds, our crew was armed and ready. If we were
indeed where I thought we were, near Xandropolis and the
sea, these visitors could be anyone at all—Rhemians, desert
raiders, or worse still—outriders of the rebel Fhazir.

They stopped, cautiously, well out of range. It was clear,
now, they were Nicieans—gaunt riders on fleet horses, faces
hidden under flowing white robes.

"What do you think?" I asked Thareesh.

"In these times, who can say? It is no longer an easy thing
to mark a friend in Niciea. Whoever they are, we can give
them something to think about."

I agreed, and as we had done once before on the other
side of Kenyarsha, we raised the royal banner of the Empire
of Niciea to our mast. The sight of that brilliant green flag
with its field of golden eyes set the somber riders cheering.
On the decks, we grinned at one another like children, for it
had been a time since the *Ahzir al'Rhaz* had dropped its sails
among friends.

The leader of this band was named Sha'desh. He was a
former captain of cavalry, had fought in the last siege of
Chaarduz, and was fiercely loyal to the Empire. When he
learned I was the foreigner who had been *rhadaz'meh* of
Lord Tharrin, brother of the king, tears welled unashamedly
in his lidless eyes.

"Then I do not have to tell you that the small prince lives,"
he said. "Niciea has bled deeply from its wounds, but in
time, it will heal and be strong again."

Sha'desh surely knew that it was a most extraordinary
thing to encounter a vessel sailing *north* toward the Southern

Sea. He was a soldier, though, and if he was curious, said nothing. Instead, he gave us sound advice as to what we could expect to meet ahead.

"The Southern Sea is no more than a day's ride from here. If you intend to pass that way, I must tell you that the coast is in Rhemian hands. There are many vessels of war offshore, and troops as far inland as Xandropolis." He paused to spit distastefully on the sand. "That city is no longer free to all peoples, as it once was. The only traders who pass those walls are Rhemians, or the scum of Fhazir. They appear to get along famously, which is not surprising."

I considered his words. "I would not imagine they watch this entrance to the Southern Sea too closely."

"No," he said, "I can tell you they do not."

"Then a swift vessel would have a fair chance of losing itself quickly in the night, and gaining open water."

Sha'desh grinned. "Better than a fair chance, Aldair. For if such a thing should happen, there would no doubt be some occurrence hereabouts that would greatly attract the Rhemians' attention."

"Such an event would be appreciated."

The captain shrugged. "We are not many, perhaps, but we make a fair amount of noise when we have to."

Dinner that evening was a pleasant affair. Sha'desh and two of his officers joined us aboard the *Ahzir*. There was plenty of wine and barley beer, and the Niceans brought a large pot of *d'shei-ashhii*, the sweet, pasty stew made of several varieties of insects, which is the national dish of the country. Thareesh, of course, was delighted, and Rhalgorn was on good behavior and said nothing about 'bug eaters.' This may have been because Signar threatend him with his life, but I prefer to think it was because the Stygiann held these soldiers in great esteem. There is little the Lords of the Lauvectii hold sacred, but they respect the honor of a warrior, be he friend or foe. Certainly, these Niceans who fought on against great odds for the love of their shattered nation, deserved whatever honor we might give them.

Who can fathom the ways of a female? Since my adventure in the Wastes, Corysia had gone to great lengths to avoid me, and it was clear she did not wish to remember what had passed between us. Perhaps she thought I was in too deep a fever to recall her endearments—or hoped that this

was so. At any rate, she graced our table with her presence
that night, and managed to be charming and polite to all—
no easy task for persons of blood and breeding. As ever, she
took great care with her appearance, though she was far from
the pots and paints and handmaidens such a person is accustomed to having about them. There was a touch of color
around her snout, and at the pink tips of her ears. The soft
light of our lamps turned her fine coat to satin, and the hairs
about her cheeks were curled in tiny ringlets. As a female of
fashion, she kept her bristles cleanly plucked—a habit I have
always found enticing.

Looking, of course, is not the same as touching—and
without the latter, the former is usually most uncomfortable.
At any rate, I decided, a romance that flourishes only under
semi-conscious conditions will probably never amount to
much.

We were all up and about well before the sun, for now
that our plans were set, there was much to do before the day
was out. There was no great need to linger in this narrow
sea. If Sha'desh and his riders could find us there, Rhemians
could do the same. We would wait for the dark, then, and
row through most of the night until we caught sight of the
Southern Sea. Sha'desh and his troops would flank us on the
shore for the greater part of this trip, then break away to the
west above Xandropolis. He assured me there were a great
many structures along the docks there that might accidentally
catch afire. When we saw flames on the horizon, we would
make for the open sea.

This was our plan, and it came about just as I have described it. The sky over the Rhemian-held shore lit up as if
the sun had fallen, giving us a great deal more light than we
really wanted. Still, we saw no Rhemian ships, and by some
miracle, none saw us. We caught a good wind and set sail west
for the Straits, and Albion.

From experience, I should have guessed that if we sailed
for one place, we would surely reach another. I have said
before that it is a great blessing we are blind to our to-
morrows.

TWENTY-FIVE

Through the rest of the night we watched a faint smudge of orange behind us, marking the brave Niceans' diversion. Closer, there was another, equally pleasing sight. To the south and east, bright points of fire paralleled our course, running just behind the speed of the *Ahzir*. Signar gave a deep grunt of satisfaction at this. "The fellow's made a fair night's work," he told us. "I can't say how, but what he's done is catch a fine nest of Rhemian shipping in the harbor, and spark 'em all to burning!"

We counted six of these doomed vessels in all, but only one stayed with us until the dawn. We saw it go under not a league away—a blackened hull with dark tangles of charred rigging on her decks. From the looks of this craft it had been a coastal runner, slimmer and faster than most of the Rhemian warships.

In the heat of battle you will hear a victorious crew loose their blood-cries upon an enemy—laughing at drowning creatures and cursing their vessel long after it has dropped beneath the waves. Now, though, there was only silence aboard the *Ahzir*, for there is no victory in such a sight.

The sun blazed suddenly out of the east, painting the gray water gold, and lighting this tragedy for all to see. Black timbers and bits of fouled line floated upon the sea. A half-burned cask bobbed to the surface a moment, then disappeared.

"I hate the devils for what they are," muttered Signar, "but it's no way for a seaman to meet his end, whoever he might be." The big Vikonen shook his head and turned away, bellowing orders to make our way west again.

We were glad enough to leave this sight behind, and every soul aboard quickly found something to do. Still, the ship was hardly underway before the lookout shouted, and brought us all to starboard. I could hardly believe my eyes, but there it was—the head and shoulders of an old seaman, just across our bow. Here is a person the gods have smiled upon, I told myself, for only great luck could bring him through such a horror alive.

Luck, though, was an ill-chosen word, for when we brought the fellow aboard it was clear that he was badly-burned, and in great pain. There was little we could do, now, except make him comfortable. Warriors have a sense about the dead and dying, for they have seen enough of both. "He will not last for long," said Thareesh.

"Not if he is lucky," added the Stygiann. "I will say a prayer to the wood gods of the Lauvectii; if they can hear me over large bodies of water, perhaps they will grant him a relatively easy death. If not," he touched the hilt of his sword, "I am not overly sensitive about such things and would be willing to do the job myself."

At that, the old seaman's eyes widened and he clawed painfully at the decking, making pitiful efforts to throw himself back into the sea. I sent Rhalgorn packing and kneeled down to offer the fellow water. "You have nothing to fear," I assured him, "you are among friends, and no harm will come to you."

He took the water eagerly, but was too frightened to speak. This is fairly understandable, under the circumstances. Even without the threat of Rhalgorn, the sight of so many free creatures of different lands must have been most confusing. In this world, people are used to seeing other races in chains, dead, or coming at them with a weapon. At any rate, he welcomed the water, and lay back upon the deck. I'm sure he would have died there without moving again if Corysia hadn't happened on the deck at that moment. At the sight of her, he jerked up on his shoulders and cried out— a dry, rattling sound that near drained his strength away.

Corysia went pale, dropped down beside him and cradled his head in her arms. Tears streamed down her cheeks and the old sailor smiled through his pain. "Aldair—" She looked up, her eyes pleading. "Can't you *do* something? He is hurt, terribly!"

"There is nothing to be done," I told her. "He is dying, Corysia."

Anger started in her features but the Rhemian stopped her. "He is right, Lady. And there's nothing more I could be wanting, now, but the sight of yourself. By the Creator, it's a thing worth dying for, I'll tell you, to see you safe and sound. We thought you'd perish, for certain—" He stopped, remembering where he was, and looked up fearfully to catch my eyes.

"It's all right, old friend," she assured him. "I am safe with these people. It is a very long story, Proctorius, and I shall tell it to you when you're better." She forced a little laugh. "I have heard more than one tall tale upon your knee, and it is high time I gave you one back—though I think you'll scarce believe it."

"Oh, I think I would, Lady," he said wearily, "if there was time to do the telling."

"You are *not* going to die," she said firmly, "I—just won't *have* it. Do you understand?"

"Yes, Lady, I do. And I wish I could follow your bidding."

"You will, then, if you wish it."

"Lady—"

"For now, though, you must rest. We have much to talk about, but it can wait. One day soon we'll be back in Rhemia together. We will sit in our favorite spot behind the garden, and you'll tell me what an old soldier is doing at sea, playing like a sailor, and I'll tell me *my* adventures. We— *Proctorius!*" Corysia closed off her cries with the back of her hand. I knelt down quickly and took her shoulders. "Corysia, I'm sorry. He's going."

"No!"

At her voice, the old Rhemian's eyes fluttered open. He was going, but not yet gone. "Lady—"

"No, don't talk."

"I—must, Lady. Listen . . . don't—go—back—to Rhemia. You must—not!"

"What? Proctorius."

He shook his head feebly to quiet her. "It's bad, Lady. There's—terrible evil afoot—spreading like a fester far and wide. Mustn't—"

I saw the very moment Death came down and breathed upon his eyes. Corysia saw it too, and covered her face and wept. She stayed there, holding the old soldier to her, until we gently eased her from him and took him below.

What he meant to say, I could not fathom, for there is always trouble in Rhemia. It is a way of life with empires, be they Rhemian or Nicean or any other. I do not think it matters whether the powers that rule these lands are well-intentioned or otherwise. The Niceans wished only the best for their people, but this did not keep the royal house from crumbling. It may well be that no great power can stand forever, that each carries within it the seeds of its own destruction. After all, even the Empire of Man, which shaped the world, is dead and gone.

Rhalgorn broke my thoughts, laying a small packet in my hands. "It was on the Rhemian," he said, "wrapped about his waist under his clothing." The packet bore the royal seal of the Empire, and was well made. Even so, the sea had done its work, and I could read only parts of the message within:

For Marcus Quintus
Commanding the Garrison
at Xandropolis

You are directed to withdr   all tr   Xandropolis and

re imm Rhemia. Bearer of the   essage
Proc   s   trus   a loyal. He wi   a and not
t ee the uni for I c n dare not pu to
pen here.   imper ive th   ee   c turmoil,
so take a ca   the usua y   traito s withi oo m
is widespread, eve through   t for   rt agents o i
heretic Fabius Domitius wh   io   re
an thro t e pr on

Magius Cal   e n
Couns l Rh   a
Dem ii 8 4 0
Br i e   o

The world turned crazily about me. I reached out, grasping for whatever might be at hand, and found the Stygiann. He stared, bewildered, then Signar and Thareesh were beside him. Still, I could find no words. What could I say? That all we had gained was likely lost? That we could not sail to Albion, for Albion had come to Rhemia? There are no words for such a moment.

"I, for one, can't make myself believe it," said the Vikonen. "That quiet and gentle fellow." He shook his head and muttered to his cup.

"That quiet and gentle fellow has betrayed us all," I told him, "and there is no use wondering if there is another who bears his name, or if there's some mistake in this!" I brought a fist down hard upon the table. "Believe me—it is the same Fabius Domitius we left on Albion. *Gentle* scholar Fabius is the *heretic* Fabius who has taken himself to Rhemia. And Creator knows what horrors he's carried with him!"

No one spoke, but I knew what they were thinking. "We don't truly know what's happened there," Signar said finally. He scratched his chest and frowned. "The old soldier's message said little."

The others looked at me, waiting, for this was in their minds, too.

"That's so," I said. "But it said enough. We don't *have* to know what he's done there to know he's a danger to us all. We know he came from Albion, and that's for certain enough for me!"

"Aldair's right," Rhalgorn admitted. "It appears that nothing good comes from that place."

I stood, facing them. "Look. If you think I make too much of this, say so. We're companions all and I welcome your words. Rhalgorn? Thareesh? And, Signar—it's true that it would be most helpful if Proctorius had told us more. But, *damn* me, what more did he *need* to say than this!" I jerked the faded message from my pocket and waved it in their faces. "Do you think the Empire calls its legions back to Rhemia for nothing?"

Thareesh looked up with lidless eyes. "I cannot say what this Fabius learned in Albion, or what has possessed him to turn against us. But Aldair speaks the truth. We need not wonder at the evil he may have brought to Rhemia. It is unnecessary to look further than the deck of the *Ahzir*."

Signar's eyes widened. "He couldn't loose a thing like that!"

"He need only be as mad as Man to try it," said Thareesh.

I looked in my cup, at the dregs of wine there. "I do not see how we can guess what he has done. We must *know*. There is nothing else for it."

No one spoke for a long moment. Finally, Signar broke the silence. "That's plain enough, Aldair, and you're as right as you can be."

"To Rhemia, then," said Rhalgorn.

"There is no other way, is there? How we'll do this, I cannot say, for there is no more deadly place on earth for us to show ourselves—"

"*I* know how it can be done, Aldair, though you do not."

I turned in my chair to see Corysia, standing in the shadow of the door. How long she had been there, I could not say.

"This is a thing that I can do," she said calmly. "Tell me where it is you wish to go, and I will take you there. For it seems that it is my land they wish to destroy now."

~~~~~~~~~~~~~~~~~~~~

TWENTY-SIX

~~~~~~~~~~~~~~~~~~~~

It is no exaggeration to say Corysia worked small miracles to get us into Rhemia. All about were signs of her youth, and each new memory served us well. She guided the *Ahzir* into a small, well-hidden cove north of the city. Even Signar was dumbfounded, for it was a place no decent harbor ought to be. Still, there it was. A seabird foreign to these waters would have passed it by—Corysia, of course, had played here as a child.

There were paths through the woods, and roads around small villages that gave us safe passage. And, in the city itself, alleys and narrow ways the meanest thief in Rhemia must have shunned.

"For a lady of royal bearing," I told her, sniffing the foul air about us, "you have a remarkable knowledge of the local sewers."

"And *you* are most fortunate, Aldair, that little girls are often less than ladies," she answered, a very disconcerting gleam in her eye. I did not pursue this, for she was clearly in the mood to tell me more than I cared to know about her youth.

"Cities," scoffed Rhalgorn, wrinkling his gray muzzle at all around him, "each is more disgusting than the last, if possible. How does a warrior know when enemies are near, if there is only the smell of garbage in the air?"

"If you are born in the cities," Thareesh explained, "it is the same. One learns the smells, as he would in a forest."

Rhalgorn, of course, did not care to believe such non-

132

sense. "It is a most unseemly place for a Stygiann," he muttered.

Our first night ashore, Corysia took us quickly through the countryside, nearly to the edge of the city itself. We waited there under a hayrack for night to fall again, while she went ahead to learn what she could. In truth, we knew next to nothing about what we were walking into. Was the Emperor Titus Augustus still in power? How strong was Fabius Domitius? Hopefully, these were questions Corysia could answer. When I put these thoughts into words, it was Signar who quickly let me know what was in his mind.

"*If* she comes back," he blurted, though he knew my feelings on this. Thareesh gave him a withering look, but it was lost on the Vikonen, and I said nothing. I was well aware that I had put our lives in the hands of the same Rhemian lady I had stolen from the streets of far Duroctium. The fact that she could easily betray us had crossed my mind more than once. I was certain, however, that she would not. Corysia had no great allegiance to us, but she loved the land of her birth—near as much, I suppose, as the rest of us despised it.

It was near to dusk when she returned. At first, we didn't recognize her—which is quite understandable, as she was dressed in the full armor of a Rhemian legionary. More than that, two good mounts trailed behind her, heavily burdened with wares and guided by a true Rhemian soldier. Thareesh was near to stitching the whole train with arrows before I stopped him.

"Good," Corysia said coolly, when I told her. "If you four heroes didn't see through the guise, perhaps no one else will either."

Corysia's follower was called Gaius. He was fiercely loyal, and would clearly do whatever she asked, but it was plain he didn't like the looks of us. He would speak to me, if necessary, but wouldn't get near my companions.

Over good ale and sausages, Corysia told her story. I had guessed, already, that she did not bear good tidings. "It is far worse than you imagined," she said. "The heretic and his forces control the heart of the city now. Many nobles have been taken or killed. The Church is in ruin, for there is where he wisely struck first. It is said that he murdered many of the Good Fathers who held high office, and that he keeps the Holy Father himself alive as a threat to those who refuse to do his bidding." Corysia's voice went hard. "In truth, it appears that he did not need to threaten *all* the citizens of Rhemia. A great many common folk and Churches alike have willingly taken up his cause, for he gives them miracles they can see. Aldair," she said bitterly, "they call him Son of the Creator!"

I sat up straight at that. "Miracles? What sort of miracles, Corysia?"

It was Gaius who answered. "I have seen these things myself, though of course—" a quick glance at Corysia, "I do not believe they are true miracles."

"Tell me. Please. Exactly what you have seen."

"When Fabius Domitius appears—which is not often, for sure—he carries a shiny metal cylinder in his hand. In the night, this thing projects a brilliant blue light for a great distance. It is like nothing you have seen before! No candle or lamp could begin to do such a thing. It is said—" Gaius went red and looked away, "—that is, the *heretic* and his followers claim this is the same blue light which once floated over—"

"—Albion," I finished, for he could not bring himself to say the word. For a person who did not believe these miracles, Gaius seemed to put a great deal of feeling into his speech.

The Rhemian told of other marvels Fabius Domitius used to awe and frighten his followers—though he did not believe these, either. There was a stick that belched thunder, and killed wherever it pointed. Capes and boots of gold and quicksilver. Even a saddle upon two metal wheels, which could be made to carry a person forward by the use of his feet. This last, as Rhalgorn would say, did not appear to be a seemly mode of travel for the Son of the Creator.

None of these wonders surprised me, for Fabius had had ample time to search the storehouses of Man below Albion. The lights, of course, I had seen in that place myself. They are truly marvelous things, but I know for certain they were a most common means of illumination in the world of Man, and no miracle at all. —But what poor citizen of Rhemia could hope to know this?

So far, it appeared that Fabius had needed only a few shiny relics to shake the Empire. I knew, though, that he was better armed than this, and I shuddered to think what he would do when the Emperor's returning legions tried to stand in his way.

Corysia told me, with shame in her voice, that even a few

nobles close to Titus Augustus had gone over to Fabius. Her father, of course, was not a person to be taken in by such folly. Gaius reported that he was in hiding outside the city where the Emperor was gathering loyal segments of the army. Sadly, even many of these hard-bitten fellows had been taken in by the heretic. I did not comment upon this, but I was not overly surprised to hear it. The Rhemian soldier has a rather alarming habit of changing leaders, and even emperors, for less than noble reasons. They seem particularly susceptible to persons with good speaking voices, and silver in their pockets.

Listening to these two, I was suddenly struck by the thought that I had been through all this once before. I vividly remembered Chaarduz, the great capital of Niciea, in flames, while nobles fled the city and wondered if the army could be trusted. Most of them, in this case, were loyal. But it made little difference in the end. The priest Bhurzal filled the people with terror, then opened the gates of the city to the rebel Fhazir.

The circumstances are not the same, of course. But they are not all that different, either.

Corysia had given much thought to the manner in which we could safely enter the city. Thus, Corysia, Gaius and I wore the garb of soldiers, while Rhalgorn, Signar and Thareesh trailed behind in chains. In this way, we easily navigated the narrow streets and foul alleys of Rhemia, to the house of Gaius the legionary. And perhaps it is some sort of commentary on the Empire and its citizens to say that even in the midst of anarchy and rebellion, we were hardly noticed, for the selling of one being to another is one of the most common trades within the city.

~~~~~~~~~~~~~~~~~~

TWENTY-SEVEN

~~~~~~~~~~~~~~~~~~

The house of Gaius was in the northern quadrant of the city, where many soldiers and tradesmen make their homes. Here, each dwelling is packed so close upon another it is near impossible to tell where one begins and the other ends. Adding to the beauty of this area is a dark and foul smelling river which carries the waste of near a quarter-million people to the sea.

Both Rhalgorn and Signar had much to say on this. In the eyes of Rhemia, Stygianns and Vikonen are crude, savage barbarians, who lack the culture and wisdom of a citizen of the Empire. In truth, however, it must be said that neither of these races build cities atop their own sewage. It is hard to come up with a fair definition of a barbarian, for wherever you go, there are differing opinions on this. Still, as best I can gather, he is a person who lives too far away to smell his nearest neighbor.

Darkness came upon us shortly after we arrived, and from the flat roof of Gaius' house we watched the troubled city struggle with itself. Cries of alarm reached us through the night. Soldiers in armor clattered over cobbled streets, and in the distance, there was the unmistakable ring of iron on iron. More than once, fires sprang up to the south, adding great yellow blossoms to the million tiny eyes of Rhemia. Smoke from these fires reached us when the wind was right, and told us what was burning. Once, amid less pleasant odors, I caught the clean scents of spice and honey.

136

"You get this many folks together in one place," Signar complained, "You can't help havin' trouble. If it wasn't one thing, it'd be something else." And no doubt, he was right.

There is a saying in the Eubirones that Mother Day puts Fear to bed. This was not so in Rhemia. Fear was very much awake that day, stalking every street and alley. The city held its breath, waiting behind shuttered windows to see what might happen next.

"What I am saying has nothing to do with how well you know the city," I argued with Corysia. "This is *not* the city you knew. It is a place full of danger and treachery, and it is just plain foolish to chance these streets."

"Aldair, Rhemia has *always* been full of treachery—and danger, too, I suppose." She flung her pretty head about, casting my words aside with the gesture. Her light-hearted manner in this made me angry, and she knew it.

"All right," she admitted finally, "it is not the best of times. But I will be careful, and Gaius will be with me. I do know the city, Aldair, and there is much we have to learn about this Fabius Domitius. You yourself have said it will be hard enough to get close to him, even with the best of help."

What she said was true, but this did not still my concern. "It would be better, I think, if I went with you."

Corysia smiled. "I—don't really think so, Aldair."

"Why not? Surely you don't think I'd appear like this, in the colors of clan Venicii. I do have the soldier's clothing."

"I know."

"Well, then?"

"It is not so much a matter of the—clothing."

"What?"

"Aldair—" She bit her lip and inspected a corner of the room. "I mean no offense, but you—simply do not *look* very much like a Rhemian."

I am slow at times, but eventually, light appears. "I see that you have not learned a great deal from your travels," I said stiffly. "You are still the fine lady."

Corysia sighed. "You're angry. And I didn't *mean* anything by that at all."

"Fine. I hope it won't surprise you to hear I have never made a great deal of effort to look like a Rhemian. Where I come from, it is not considered particularly desirable."

There was more to this conversation, but I see no need to

record it. Since we'd set our course for Rhemia, I had
imagined—and hoped—I saw the beginnings of a different,
more amenable Corysia. Evidently, the original model was
still with us. Finally, she left, trailing Gaius, and an icy
silence, behind her. We barbarians were left to fend for
ourselves.

This was no easy matter, for the four of us were caged
together in those small, stuffy quarters so prized by the city
dwellers, with nothing to do but wait. There was wine to
drink, but it was the cheap, sour stuff the taverns save for
soldiers, because they will buy it without complaining. In
addition, we had a plentiful supply of flies. That is one
thing about Rhemia—even the pooerst citizens has all the
flies he could ask for.

"I cannot believe I would ever say such a thing," muttered
Rhalgorn, pouring the dregs of his cup over the stone
floor, "but I *miss* that damnable boat. It is unseemly to float
about on great pieces of water, but at least the air is fit
to breathe."

"Ship," Signar said dully. "It is a ship, Stygiann, not a
boat."

Rhalgorn ignored him. "Of course, if I could be anywhere
I wished, I would be snaring rabbits in the woods of the
Lauvectii, on a fine summer day. That, now, is the greatest of
all pleasures." His red eyes gleamed, and his thick tail
trembled at the thought.

"I will tell you something *I* cannot believe," I said. "I
would rather be snaring rabbits *with* you than stuck in this
hovel in the middle of Rhemia."

Rhalgorn grinned and showed his teeth; the picture of a
warrior of the Venicii tracking hares with a Stygiann greatly
amused him.

How long had Corysia been gone, I wondered? It seemed
like half a day or more, but it could not have been more
than an hour. Bad wine and the stuffy little room had taken
its toll. Signar lay half asleep in a corner, for there was no
stool in the place big enough to hold his bulk. Rhalgorn
slumped beside the door to the alley, eyes half-closed, gray
furry ears limp against his head. A circle of flies buzzed
happily 'round his nose. Thareesh was up the narrow stairs
and on the roof, keeping watch there.

And I? I have tried, but I cannot remember exactly what
I was doing at the time. To this day, I have only bits and

pieces of the picture. I remember hearing something. I remember forcing one eye open, then another, and thinking it was not at all like the quiet and graceful Thareesh to come tumbling and shrieking down the stairs like a drunken farmer. Suddenly, I was fully awake. Thareesh was curled like a cord about Rhemian armor, his knife flashing red. Rhalgorn was a flash of gray murder. Rhemians were thick as marshflies in the room and I was groping for a sword that wasn't there. Signar's roar split the air and a great black fist came down to flatten a crested helm. Then, some oaf of a fellow was pounding me with something hard and breathing garlic in my face, and I thought how foolish it was to leave a blade across the room where it was little help to anyone.

~~~~~~~~~~~~~~~~~~~

TWENTY-EIGHT

~~~~~~~~~~~~~~~~~~~

Very few people have the opportunity to wake in a standing position. It is a frightening, unpleasant sensation. My feet hung loose, floating just above the floor. I could neither see nor feel my arms. I guess they were somewhere above me, out of sight. There was a dull, tingling ache in my shoulders, and a throbbing pain at the back of my head. I tasted copper, choked, and spit blood.

"Well, Aldair, you're back with us."

It did not surprise me to find Fabius Domitius standing there before me. I had not imagined it would be anyone else. He had changed little since I left him on Albion. In spite of his new high station, he was still a short and pudgy fellow with a longish snout and heavy bristles about his jowls. Perhaps I had expected silken robes and flashing rings now that he'd sacked the treasures of Rhemia. Instead, he was simply Fabius the scholar, in common robe and cowl. Perhaps the image of poverty coupled with fearsome power better suited the Son of the Creator. The one addition to his costume undoubtedly added much to his stature—from a golden chain about his waist hung one of the infamous "godlights" Gaius had described.

"I would like to say that I am pleased to see you, Fabius, but I cannot," I told him. "What have you done with my companions? For your sake, I hope they are alive and well. You have a great many debts to pay, scholar. You had best not gain too many more!"

Fabius did not appear to be listening. He stood with his

hands behind his back, his brow creased in thought. "This is an interesting point," he said finally, looking up at me. "Debts, now. To whom, then, should I be indebted? That's the heart of the matter. To the Creator? I no longer think that such a being exists, Aldair. If he does, he is surely not *our* Creator, is he? We know our makers—you showed them to me, on Albion. Is it to them that I should hold myself accountable?" He shook his head. "No, I think we owe them nothing for the curse of creation. Who does that leave for debts, then—my fellow beasts? You cannot wrong a thing that has neither a soul nor a destiny of its own. So, that leaves only me for an accounting." He smiled. "And I have learned to live with Fabius Domitius."

"A fine, scholarly justification," I said, "but I am not one of your students, Fabius. Was this your reasoning, when you murdered Quintus, and Ambiir, and the others?" It was a guess, but one that struck home, for his eyes narrowed slightly before he caught himself. Knowing what he had become, it was not hard to imagine what he had done with his fellow scholars on Albion. The thought of this chilled me to the bone. If he had killed his friends, how could I hope that he'd spare Rhalgorn, and the others?

He watched me, and for a moment I thought I read genuine concern in his eyes. "You seem determined to anger me, Aldair. There doesn't have to be conflict between us."

I had to laugh at that. "And what would you see in this relationship? I'm strung up here like a hare in the market, and you're plainly the butcher!"

"You don't have to hang there. I'd make you comfortable if you would give me your word—"

"You have more than my word," I assured him. "You have my solemn *oath*, Fabius, that if you let me down from this thing I'll happily slit your throat."

Fabius sighed and shook his head. "I'm sorry, Aldair. I truly hoped that we could talk. I would even offer you a wine. There are some goods wines in the city, if you know where to look—though nothing made here locally seems worth the bother." With that, he turned and walked quickly away, stepping in that peculiar manner scholars seem to affect, as if they are ever moving with great urgency toward some new bit of wisdom. He stopped before a broad window, and stared out upon the day.

From the color of light, I guessed it was nearly dusk. The room about me was hight and narrow, faced on every side with dark-veined marble. The ceiling vaulted overhead in shadow, for there was only the single window I could see. The place was bare of furniture, save a simple wooden stool I assumed Fabius had brought with him.

That stool spoke volumes to me, for it was a mirror of Fabius himself. I could almost wish he'd show the fiery eyes of a fanatic, or the arrogance of a madman who would bring the world to its knees. I could understand that. There is always an ample supply of tyrants on hand, and though I am sure they would not wish to think so, they are as hard to tell apart as a roomful of farmers or millers. This Fabius, though, had none of this about him. He was a sad, lonely little fellow better suited to his books than the murder of an empire. And there, of course, was the danger in him. A tyrant lusts for power. But what did Fabius Domitius want with the world? I could not say. I could only wonder what deadly toys he'd found below Albion, and what he intended to do with them. And, I could not forget that I had led him there.

When he came back from the window, he eased himself to his stool, dropped his hands to his knees and looked at me. "Even if you do not wish to talk, Aldair, I am afraid we must. There are things I want to hear from you."

Well, it comes, then, I told myself. "I can think of nothing you'd care to know, Fabius."

"I will think of things for you, then. It has been a while since we saw one another. I would hear what you've been about."

"It is not a pleasant story," I told him, "but you can hear it if you wish. We set about to find the site of Man to the East. You are aware of this, as we planned it together. Unfortunately, we never got there. A storm hit us off Tarconii, and we never made the Straits. The *Ahzir* went down with most of the crew. Those that didn't perish are scattered to the winds, having lost their interest in the sea. As I have, by the way."

Fabius looked disappointed. "Aldair, I do not believe this story."

"I'm sorry. If I had known we'd meet in Rhemia, I would have saved a tatter of sail for you."

Fabius stood and ran a hand over his face. "This is all so useless, Aldair, such a foolish waste of time."

"Can I ask a question?"

"What?"

"*Why* did you do this, Fabius? I would honestly like to

know. Clearly, I made the greatest mistake of my life taking you to Albion, but I have yet to guess what happened to you there."

Fabius sat down again, smiling to himself. "Aldair, you think, but you do not think clearly. You know what we are, yet you insist on raising us to some high station. You sent me to Albion to learn. I did. I learned that we are beasts, plain and simple. Neither better nor worse than our makers."

"Not yet, perhaps," I reminded him, "but we can be."

He waved me aside. "I am tired of that dream—how we will work together to turn the tide of history. Reason and logic does not move the world. I have walked the scholar's path, and there is nothing on it." He looked up. "To answer your question, I did what I did because I was tired of what I was doing." He spread his hands. "Nothing more, though I don't expect you to believe that. I saw the threads of my destiny. I saw that whatever I did—or anyone did—didn't matter. I don't particularly want to be an emperor, as you might have guessed. It seems a lot of bother, to be honest. Still, if I am on this path, why, that's the path I was *meant* to take, since nothing can be changed in this world."

"You don't believe that," I told him. "You've twisted reason to fit your needs, Fabius. I'm damned if you don't make a better tyrant than a thinker!"

Fabius looked amused. "Aldair. Do you *know* this isn't the history they planned for us? That somewhere down in Albion there's not a picture we could play upon one of those marvelous windows—one that would show the both of us, just as we are at this moment? You trussed up on a stick and me standing before you? Wouldn't it be the perfect joke of Man, letting his poor creatures think they've broken free?"

Certainly, in moments of despair, this thought had crossed my mind.

"Well, then—" He waved a finger at me. "I see it in your eyes, Aldair. You have thought upon it."

"What you're saying is plain foolishness."

"Is it? How do you know I haven't seen those pictures myself?"

"Because they're not there to see."

Fabius stood. He sighed deeply, clasped his hands together, then dropped them at his side. "Ah, Aldair, that is one of the joys of the ignorant, I suppose. They are so sure of everything." He leaned down and rapped his stool against the floor. Somewhere behind me, a door opened. Bootsteps clattered on stone paving, a blade sliced the rope about my hands and I dropped to the floor. I didn't wish to cry out when the blood climbed back into my arms, but there was nothing I could do to stop it. Soldiers on either side pulled me roughly to my feet and began dragging me across the room. Fabius stopped them, as we passed the window. I looked out. There was a courtyard, and a high wall behind it. Above the wall, a dying sun pinked the city. The crew of the *Ahzir* stood in the courtyard, bound, and chained to one another. Before them, stood the box.

Something died inside me.

"We will play no more games with one another," said Fabius. "I have already learned how you came upon this thing, and what it can do. I think I know what it is, as well."

"Fabius—I will gladly tell you all I know about it because you *must* understand what it is. You think you know, but you do not."

He gazed at the courtyard, then back to me. "I do, though, Aldair. I understand it very well."

I tried to speak as calmly as possible. Nothing was more important now than to make him listen, and believe. "You do *not*, Fabius. I know what you're thinking. It can't be used to control others. *Because it cannot be controlled itself.* You must not go near it, or attempt to open it. Please, *listen* to me on this!"

"I have," he said simply, "and now I am finished, Aldair. There is nothing more we have to say."

TWENTY-NINE

It would not have surprised me in the least if I had been taken from the room and hung without ceremony, or simply dispatched with a blade and flung into the streets. Instead, my legionaries pushed me down a narrow stairs and tossed me into the dark. A door clanged shut with great finality; a key turned heavily in the ancient lock. There was straw on the damp floor, and whole armies of vermin. A torch burned faintly in the hall outside. Only a few pale beams crept through the heavy panels. The place stank to high heaven, like all the sewers in the world brought together. If I was to die here, I hoped it would be soon, and that my snout would go first.

"*Aldair?*"

I near jumped out of my skin. "Creator's Eyes, who's that!"

"All of us, I suppose, now that you've seen fit to join us." This, followed by that peculiar hollow cough that is a Stygiann's way of laughter.

"Rhalgorn! By damn, all of you, and alive!"

"We never thought to see you," Signar said solemnly, "nor anyone else, for that matter."

"I can hardly see him now," said the Stygiann, "even with superior eyes. I am certain he is here, though, for a number of my fleas have just departed to greet the new arrival."

"Thareesh?"

"I am here, somewhere—or what is left of me. You will excuse me if I do not stand."

"Thareesh, you're hurt—"

"He is," Signar answered, "but he'll survive, as will we all, I suppose, for all the good it'll do. We are a bit worse for wear, with various bits of meat and muscle missing, and uncountable bruises. Still, there are several Rhemian soldiers who are the worse for that they gave, being somewhat dead and cold."

"And you," asked the Niciean, "are you in one piece, or more?"

"One, though I expect my arms are somewhat longer than they were." I told them all that had happened to me with Fabius, and what had passed between us, though I could hardly bring myself to say the box was in his hands, and our crew all prisoners.

When I was finished, no one spoke for a long moment. "Our crew, the ship—*every*thing?" Signar asked finally.

"Everything, it seems, old friend."

The Vikonen made a noise deep within his throat. "It was the female, Aldair. I am sorry to say it, but there is no other answer I can see. She has betrayed us."

"You do not know this for certain," hissed the Niciean. "You are buried in the ground somewhere and cannot say what is happening where you are not!"

The moment I awoke and found myself in the hands of Fabius Domitius, I tried to cast this thought from my mind. Clearly, there was little use deceiving myself longer. "If you are trying to spare my feelings, Thareesh, I am grateful. It may well be that Signar is right. If he is, I hope that I shall never know it."

"Well, damn me," rasped the Stygiann, "if you three are quite finished bemoaning our fate, and who's to blame, it might be well to get on with the business of removing ourselves from this stinkhole. I can't speak for the rest of you, but it is a most unseemly atmosphere for a Lord of the Lauvectii."

"Lord, is it?" growled the Vikonen. He moved about restlessly in the dark. "I trust his lordship's got some brilliant plan in mind, for I'm most anxious to hear it."

"I'm thinking," said Rhalgorn.

"Well, that's a rare treat for us all."

"Be patient, fat-fur. Something will come to me."

"When it does, I hope it's got a fine big haunch of Northland stag attached, and a keg or two of ale. Next to escaping from Rhemian sewers, those are the two things I like the best."

There was water in the room, if you could call it that. But no food. And none had arrived since the three were imprisoned there.

"If we—weren't to get out," asked Signar, "and I'm not saying we won't, you understand, what do you figure this scholar has in mind for us, Aldair?"

"I would not like to guess, Signar. Once I thought I knew Fabius Domitius, but I was gravely wrong. Remind me never to trust anyone with learning again."

"We can hardly afford to wait and see," remarked Thareesh. "If he had you on this rack before, he may well invite you back—or the lot of us."

"No," I shook my head, "I truly don't think so, Thareesh. As I have said, he is a most peculiar madman—a scholar turned tyrant. Ordinary kings and conquerors are generally both cruel and ignorant. Fabius is neither. Courtiers will have a hard time of it in his new empire, for I can't believe he'll ever listen to anyone but himself. He as much as told me that he didn't care to talk to me again. I don't think he'll put any of us to torture for the sheer pleasure of it."

"That's a comfort," said Signar, who had been listening carefully to all this.

"On the other hand," I added, "he is as cold as the Northern Sea, and he would give the order to murder us, with no ill feeling, if he decided we were a menace, or of no more use to him alive."

"*That's* no comfort at all," growled Signar. "Keep thinking, Stygiann."

We were *all* doing a great deal of thinking, for certain. It seemed most advisable to remove ourselves from that place before the decision was taken out of our hands.

How, though?

Even in desperate straits, a creature's mind and body betray him. None of us intended to sleep, but sleep we did. Neither vermin, foul odor, nor good intentions could prevent it.

I woke, once, and heard the boots of a guard scrape by. Again, Rhalgorn growled in his dreams and brought me up straight. What time was it? I had come here at sundown. Was the night still on us—or was it another day outside? With neither sight nor sound to spark our senses, an hour or a minute had no meaning. It may have been half the night again when I awoke once more. Something, or someone . . .

Signar's big hand came down, pressing me to silence. Again, a scratching, behind the door. A key turned quietly in the lock. Then—nothing.

"Aldair, if you or Rhalgorn or any of the others are in there, it's *me*. When I open this thing, I do not want a whole herd of great oafs tumbling down upon me."

"Corysia!" I nearly shouted out her name. The door opened, and limned against yellow light was Corysia, huddled under cloak and cowl. I ran to hold her to me, forgetting all else. Rhalgorn slipped past me, searching the dark hall with Stygiann eyes.

"Corysia—" I gazed at her in wonder, her fine features blurring with the sudden haze before my eyes. "Corysia, we—we—"

"Hush," she said, putting a finger to my lips, "I am sure you have a great many questions, and I doubt that I can give good answers to them all. Anyway, there is little time for that now." She stopped, took a breath, and let her eyes rest on each of us. "I am relieved to find you all alive. Truly. I was certain you would be, but—" She broke off, grinning. "Yes, you too, Rhalgorn." She reached out to touch him and the Stygiann's eyes went wide. For once, he had nothing to say.

"I know you, now," she told him gently. "I know you, and I do not fear you anymore."

Signar laughed, digging Rhalgorn painfully in the side. "Isn't anyone really fears his lordship here. We just tell him they do, to make him feel some better."

"Huh!" growled the Stygiann.

"Lady," Signar began, having some difficulty meeting her eyes, "I'll say it, because I have to. It was me that thought you—well, that—"

Corysia frowned at him severely, a look that softened to a smile. "I know what you thought, Signar. You need not tell me." She shook her head wearily. "I cannot say who betrayed you. Gaius was taken, soon after we left. I escaped, but not by much. I simply don't know whether they were waiting by design, or merely happened on us. From what I have learned, Aldair, I don't think the tyrant needs any traitors among our own. His eyes and ears are everywhere, eager to seek his favor." She trembled, and I held her closer.

In truth, Corysia had learned a great deal in so short a time. She knew our crew was taken, and guessed where they might be held. She had reached her father outside the city, and though he didn't pretend to understand why his daughter had taken up the cause of her kidnappers, he was too relieved to find her alive to doubt her words. I am sure she was careful to explain there was more at stake here than our lives; that Fabius now held the fate of Rhemia in his hands. At any rate, he promised he would get to the Emperor and gain his help, though this was a difficult thing to do, now—even if your wife happened to be blood sister to that person.

"Whatever happens," Corysia told us, "he will come himself with what strength he can, but I fear it will not go far against Fabius Domitius, without the aid of Titus Augustus."

She was right, of course. And I wondered how much we could hope to gain from Augustus on this? Who could blame the Emperor of the Rhemians for looking with distaste on such a plan? We were sworn enemies of the Empire, and would likely seem no different in his eyes than Fabius Domitius.

We all went quiet again as Rhalgorn signalled someone was coming down the hallway. "They are ours," Corysia assured him. "For the moment, at least." She glanced scornfully over her shoulder. "They are bought and paid for, and will see us out of here, but we can trust them no further than that. Outside, we will count upon our own."

Signar, Rhalgorn and Thareesh conferred briefly in the hall, and we had a small moment to ourselves. "Corysia, we cannot say what will come of this," I began.

"I know what's in your mind, Aldair," she said gently, "for you are in my thoughts, as well. I think we have much to say to one another."

I looked into her eyes, then, and saw that this was so—for there were fires within that I had never seen before. "We will have to get through this thing," I told her, "for I intend to learn those thoughts, Corysia—each and every one."

THIRTY

Chill gusts of midnight air were more than welcome after the fetid breath of our cell. The city was blessedly dark, except for a few small fires far behind the rooftops. Our helpers scuttled quickly away, as soon as they could. With pay in their pockets, they wanted nothing more to do with us. Rhalgorn and Thareesh were all for making sure they didn't go straight to Fabius for another boon, but Corysia wouldn't have it.

We waited, in the shadow of a high wall. As my eyes grew accustomed to the dark, I saw it was the very wall that held the courtyard below Fabius' window. Looking up, I saw that single port stare back, a dark and empty eye.

After a near eternity, shadows moved across the courtyard, and Corysia's friends came up to join us. She hurried to meet them, and after silent direction, Signar disappeared with half a dozen soldiers to free the rest of our crew, held in another quarter of the building.

Corysia came back, leading a tall Rhemian behind her. "You two have met, I believe, under slightly different circumstances." I caught the faint hint of hesitation in her voice, and wondered at it, until his face came close enough to see. She was right. We knew each other, but not well. His name was Marcus Sabinus, and I had last seen him watching me from a rocky point, as we sailed from Gaullia. Before that, I had fought him in the forests of Duroctium, after stealing Corysia from his charge.

"You said we would meet again," I told him, "and we

have. I'm sure this is no more to your liking than mine, but we are grateful for your help."

"You may thank the Lady for my presence," he said, pulling himself up stiffly. "I would meet you in a different manner, but for her."

"Marcus—"

The soldier turned on her sharply. "Lady, you know I do your bidding, and your father's. You must not ask for more than that!"

Corysia went silent. I spoke to him of our plans—how it was most important to seize Fabius, if we could, though there were greater needs at hand. When I mentioned the metal box Fabius had taken, his face went blank. He left us, had words with one of his officers, and returned. "There is word of a treasure the heretic guards closely, though it may not be the same as you describe." He studied me coolly. "Is this truly of great value? I ask, because if it is to be gained, lives will be lost in the taking."

"It is not a treasure," I explained. "It is a thing that will allow Fabius Domitius to destroy your land, and all its people, if he wishes. I cannot tell you how this could be, but it is true."

Marcus glanced at Corysia, then nodded shortly at me. "It is there," he pointed, "in that tower. Heavily guarded. We can take the sentries outside—but those within will know it, and sound the alarm. None of this will gain us much, however, for we could not storm the place with anything less than seige engines. It is too sturdily built for a handful of soldiers with no equipment."

"We will have to find a way!" I told him.

He looked at me with some small hint of respect. "Then, I suppose we will."

With the crew back safely, our numbers swelled, but we had few weapons between us. Only Marcus' soldiers were armed for fighting.

"We will remedy that," said Signar. "There will be those before us who will not be needing theirs." Rhalgorn's red eyes answered him in the dark.

Marcus Sabinus was right, as far as he knew. The keep where the Sentinel of Man lay guarded was indeed near impregnable. However, its builders had not reckoned with the agility of Nicieans, who can climb like roaches up nearly anything another race can build. We watched Thareesh and two companions slip by the sentries below, and disappear up the side of the tower. We saw them no more, but I knew they were there, slim forms flat against stone, slithering from one hold to another where no such hold should be.

Marcus watched all this in silence, and I would have given much to know his mind. Corysia stayed close beside me, hands grasped tightly on my arm. This did not go unnoticed, and it was clearly not to the Rhemian's liking. I cannot say whether Corysia was aware of his feelings, but I'm certain they went somewhat beyond the bounds of duty.

No sound came from the tower. Nicieans do not make a great deal of noise at any time, and less when they are bringing blood. When the heavy door swung open before us, we were ready for it. The sentries did not expect to see green-scaled warriors pouring out of their own safe tower, and we took them quickly from two sides, the Nicieans accounting for their share.

While we held the keep, Marcus Sabinus led a small force to the stables and found it lightly guarded. Soon, we had eight horses and a cart which would hold the heavy metal cannister. Though we were not much of a match for any real opposition, we were armed, and greatly strengthened in spirit.

And none too soon, for certain. A cry from our own guards brought us all alive. A detachment of Fabius' soldiers was cutting one of our patrols to pieces past the tower. They were nearly done for before we could reach them.

"I figured things were getting too peaceful," growled Signar. He hefted a big war axe in his fist and loped after Rhalgorn across the courtyard. I shouted them back.

"We won't run from a fight if it finds us," I said, "but we can't let them take us here—not with the box!"

Rhalgorn nodded, reluctantly. His sword was already well blooded. "Our little warrior is right, Vikonen. Without help, we'll not last long in this place."

Marcus Sabinus clattered up beside us, his mount striking sparks on stone. He was a seasoned legionary, and knew our odds. "We're forming up there," he panted grimly. "Get your people together quickly. Another minute and we'll be boxed like mice in a barrel." Iron clanged behind him and he was gone.

Fabius' soldiers were fully awake, now. They swarmed into the courtyard yelling for blood, and finding plenty to spill. With a short cry and a wave of his sword, Marcus led us out the gates and through the cobbled streets. Those on foot took the point, with our cart behind them, while the few of us with mounts held the enemy at bay as best we could. This came to little enough, and we were soon in full retreat through Rhemia. A legionary went down beside me, an arrow in his throat. I turned my mount to aid a big Vikonen crewman, but soldiers drove me back. The last I saw of the poor fellow was a broad and burly back, wet with red. From the howls around him, I was sure he'd take more than one of our foes down with him.

"The bridge!" Marcus bellowed in my ear, "if help's to come, it'll come from there!" He was off again, scattering armor before his great mount. I peered in his direction, but saw nothing. A shadow loomed up and I cut it down. We fought in darkness, wreaking terrible, bloody carnage, with no sure way to mark friend from foe. Someone shook me from behind—I turned, nearly slashing out at Rhalgorn. His face was torn and bloody, but he was alive, and mounted, Corysia clinging to him, eyes wide with fear. His words were lost in the din of battle, but I looked where he was pointing. The bridge! A high arc of stone stretched over a lower sector of the city, and on the other side—nothing. I knew, then, we would see no help across that span, for none was coming. Perhaps the Emperor himself stopped Corysia's father. Or Fabius cut him off some other way. He could be fighting for his life a city block away and we would never hear his cries above our own.

Someone torched the streets behind us. Fire leaped up to light the sky. The tyrant's troopers shouted at this, and came to meet us. Flames topped their helms and danced upon their swords. Once, I glanced behind and found Corysia. Rhalgorn had placed her by the cart, well in the center of the bridge. She was alive, then, and the Man-thing still in our hands. What would it serve us, though, if we all died there beside it?

There was no more time for thinking. A soldier was upon me, then another. Iron met my own, and nearly numbed me to the shoulder. I hammered the fellow on his shield, then kicked it aside and took him in the ribs. It was no clean thrust, but it felled him. Suddenly, pain cut my leg and sent me reeling. I howled, jerked down, and plucked a short red dagger hanging there. Iron stung my shoulder and I was down, staring at the sky. My mount loomed above, screaming out his life, his belly ripped away.

I saw Rhalgorn wreaking murder, his motions near too fast to follow. Signar stood black and terrible against the greater dark, Rhemians clinging to his hide like leeches. He shook them off with a fury, the silver axe in his fist cutting paths of flesh aside.

A short, stocky soldier flung himself at me like a storm. I staggered, fell, pulled myself up, and he was on me again. His face came up to mine and I looked into a single black eye, an ugly scar across a crooked snout. This one wanted me badly. I hacked away until I thought my arm would drop and still he came. It was much like raining blows upon a tree with a sack. He was not alone, now. His fellows smelled blood and came in for the kill.

Somewhere, Marcus Sabinus gave a raw cry against the night, but I never heard his words. My great stout oak and his saplings pressed upon me. Red clouded my eyes. I shook my head, slinging blood and flesh away. One more blow would do it, I thought, one—or maybe half of that. I was down, then, and they were on me, awful grins stretching their faces.

"Rheif!"

No, I remembered, Rheif was dead, at peace beneath the earth.

"Rhalgorn! Signar, to me!"

My mouth made words, but nothing came. The oak trees grinned above, shifted his blade for the blow. The grin went slack. His one dark eye went wide and a cry stuck in his throat. His fellows backed away, staring. One dropped his blade, then another. Soldiers close at hand who had no part in our fray went white and threw their swords to ground and fled.

I saw it, then, for it stood there just above me—a pale, dully-shimmering thing, like fireflies swarming on a summer's night. Again, as it had before, it looked at me and made to speak, but said nothing. It was me—and not me. It wavered, brightened, paled again, then took a step as if its feet were not upon this world at all.

At the time, I did not stop to wonder how this Aldair specter came to be. It was there, and for the moment, I was clearly without foes. Grabbing my blade, I stumbled to my feet and ran. Rhalgorn caught me at the bridge. "Corysia, Thareesh? The others?"

"I don't know!" he shouted. "Dead, alive—Aldair, there's nothing here—" He staggered, pulled himself up and gripped my arm, urging me to the bridge.

"No!" I shook him off. "We can't—leave them here!"

"Who!" He turned on me savagely. "Leave *who*, Aldair? They're dead, gone—every one!"

I wasn't listening any more. I was away from him, fighting back toward the din of battle, calling Corysia's name—but I could not move against that bloody wall.

"Corysia!"

A terrible cry rose up before me. A horde of Fabius' soldiers broke our lines and swept down upon us. Defenders rushed to fill the gap, but there was nothing else for it. It was over, and we knew it. I braced myself as best I could, raised my blade, and waited.

"Aldair!"

Corysia's voice reached out and found me, as if no other sound was there to stop it. I turned, saw her—behind me near the middle of the bridge. My blood went cold. I moved, but I knew that I would never get there. That it would happen, and nothing I could do would stop it. The driver of our cart was dead, the horse near crazed with fright. It jerked the cart wildly about, slamming first one side of the bridge, then the other. Corysia leaped for the reins; the beast pawed air and tossed her aside. Foam flecked its jaws and its eyes went white. Then, with a last, terrible shriek of fear, it shattered the wooden railing and plunged out of sight. A wheel wobbled crazily, spun from its shaft. The cart ground stone, hung for the barest second over nothing, then toppled into darkness.

I stood there in the midst of chaos, doing nothing. For there was nothing I could do now but wait for the end of the world. . . .

EPILOGUE

At dawn this day, a sun the color of lemon touched the iron-gray sea. To the north, a smudge of lampblack brushed the horizon, and I knew we were passing the far coast of Rhemia. Few ships sail the seas these days, and those that do run clear of that shore. For it is a dead place now, a desert of empty streets, and windows that look out upon nothing.

Many stories are told of that great capital of the Rhemians, and some of them are true. A trader claims that far beyond the ring of fear, one can look toward the city and see great horrors writhe above its towers. I am sure this is so. Whatever apparitions hide in a creature's heart, he can find them in that place, for the dim red eye of Man lies open in its streets.

I have heard the broken shards of empire are coming together again, to the north of the boot, near Gaullia. This may be so, but I doubt that much will come of it. Rhemia made too many enemies in its prime. Its foes have waited long to taste this moment.

I have played no small part, now, in bringing about the fall of two great civilizations. I cannot say the things that happened would not have happened without me. Still, one cannot help but wonder. If I had not left the University at Silium, and fallen into the hands of Niceans? If I had turned aside at Duroctium, and never seen Corysia? There is little point in pursuing these fancies. As we say in the Eubirones, it is impossible to pee last Thursday. One must handle such matters today.

156

However all this came about, I know for certain it was not in the plan of Man. Fabius Domitius was wrong. This rebellion of ours has *not* been written in the magic windows of Albion. If I believed this, it would be pointless to go on living in such a world.

Twice, now, I have met the ghost of myself. I do not understand this, but it happened. Thus, it has a place in this chronicle. Not surprisingly, it is Rhalgorn who has finally turned my thoughts to words on this. Stygianns are close to the gods of the earth, and know a great many things they seldom talk about. "There are worlds and times that mingle with our own," he has told me. Perhaps this is so. And will there be a time when I am that other self that appeared before me? Where, then, will be the Aldair I am now? Rhalgorn has no answer for this, nor do I.

The Stygiann has been little changed by our ventures. He is scarred about the head and chest, and his long gray muzzle seems slightly askew. But it is hard to change a Stygiann, while he is yet alive.

Thareesh suffered a painful wound upon his thigh, and lost a very small portion of his tail—though to hear him, you would think the whole of it was gone. As for Signar, there are great bare patches on his pelt where fur will never grow again, and he has nearly lost the use of his good right arm. His strength, though, is undiminished, and I would guess he can swing an axe left-handed better than any five creatures he will ever come against.

Corysia has her scars like the rest of us, though she did not wield a weapon in Rhemia. They are small scars, and do nothing to mar her beauty in my eyes. —Or in the eyes of Rhalgorn, who loves her in his own peculiar way. He would not admit this under torture, but I would not care to be nearby if any creature wrongs her.

For myself, I lost an ear, though I have no idea when this occurred. My companions have offered many useful suggestions on this subject, most of which entail cutting off the other so my head will be in balance.

It is a miracle, of course, that any of us are yet alive, for most of the *Ahzir's* crew did not survive that battle on the bridge, or the storm of fear that followed. I suppose we were all near to madness when we left that hellish place behind; it will take some doing to put that night away. I cannot say what happened to our foes, or to brave Marcus Sabinus and his followers. Some escaped, no doubt, as we did. But pitifully few creatures left that city.

Corysia has never mentioned her father, nor have I.

I wish that I could say I am wiser for my adventures. That I have come to greater understanding of the treachery of Man. Every triumph seems to turn to tragedy in my hands, and I can't see there is much that I have gained. It may be, in the end, these things will all be to the good, but it is hard to see that now.

One thing lightens my heart, as we sail for the Straits and the open sea beyond. It has been a time since I truly felt my seer was close at hand. Last night, in a dream, I think he stood beside me. I saw myself in a place I have never been before. It was a great, vast land, west past Albion, across the Misty Sea. I know that such a place is there. I saw it once in the milky sphere I found among the Avakhar, and lost again. I am certain this object showed the true shape of the world, and that the *Ahzir* will not fall off into nothing. Signar agrees with me on this, though Rhalgorn is not so sure.

For now, there is a good sea breeze in our sails, and foam beneath our prow. There is time for barley beer, good companions, and other most pleasant diversions. It is hard to imagine that every creature on Earth does not find joy in these things. Yet, many would scorn them for something less, while others would ask for more. Truly, I believe it is near impossible to satisfy everybody. . . .

Presenting JOHN NORMAN in DAW editions . . .

☐ **SLAVE GIRL OF GOR.** The eleventh novel of Earth's orbital counterpart makes an Earth girl a puppet of vast conflicting forces. The 1977 Gor novel. (#UJ1285—$1.95)

☐ **TRIBESMEN OF GOR.** The tenth novel of Tarl Cabot takes him face to face with the Others' most dangerous plot— in the vast Tahari desert with its warring tribes.
(#UE1296—$1.75)

☐ **MARAUDERS OF GOR.** The ninth novel of Tarl Cabot's adventures takes him to the northland of transplanted Vikings and into direct confrontation with the enemies of two worlds. (#UE1295—$1.75)

☐ **HUNTERS OF GOR.** The eighth novel in the saga of Tarl Cabot on Earth's orbital counterpart reaches a climax as Tarl seeks his lost Talena among the outlaws and panther women of the wilderness. (#UE1294—$1.75)

☐ **IMAGINATIVE SEX.** A study of the sexuality of male and female which leads to a new revelation of sensual liberation. (#UJ1146—$1.95)

DAW BOOKS are represented by the publishers of Signet and Mentor Books, THE NEW AMERICAN LIBRARY, INC.

☐ **ALDAIR IN ALBION** by Neal Barrett, Jr. Adrift on the
  Seas of Paradise Lost.   (#UY1235—$1.25)

☐ **WALKERS ON THE SKY** by David J. Lake. Three worlds in
  one was the system there—until the breakthrough!
                                        (#UY1273—$1.25)

☐ **THE RIGHT HAND OF DEXTRA** by David J. Lake. It's the
  green of Terra versus the purple of that alien world—with
  no holds barred.   (#UW1290—$1.50)

☐ **THE GAMEPLAYERS OF ZAN** by M. A. Foster. It's a game
  of life and death for both humans and their own creation
  —the not-quite-super race.   (#UJ1287—$1.95)

☐ **EARTHCHILD** by Doris Piserchia. Was this the only true
  human left on Earth . . . and who were the monsters that
  contended for this prize?   (#UW1308—$1.50)

☐ **DIADEM FROM THE STARS** by Jo Clayton. She became
  the possessor of a cosmic treasure that enslaved her
  mind.   (#UW1293—$1.50)

DAW BOOKS are represented by the publishers of Signet
and Mentor Books, THE NEW AMERICAN LIBRARY, INC.

THE NEW AMERICAN LIBRARY, INC.,
P.O. Box 999, Bergenfield, New Jersey 07621

Please send me the DAW BOOKS I have checked above. I am enclosing
$_____(check or money order—no currency or C.O.D.'s).
Please include the list price plus 35¢ a copy to cover mailing costs.

Name_____

Address_____

City_____State_____Zip Code_____
         Please allow at least 4 weeks for delivery